Prophesy

By L.T. World

Printed in the United States of America

FIRST EDITION

ISBN: 978-0-9977949-6-0

Published by:

Crave Press

www.cravepress.com

Dedication

For the person who first inspired me to write - Mr. Landis.

Chapter 1

Climbing a small tree that's only a few feet taller than me, I reach for the branch I commonly sit on. I don't climb this tree often, but when I'm bored with nothing better to do, I do as such. Most people at the age of fifteen practice swordsmanship, wrestle, work on a farm, or go to school if they are wealthy enough. I hate swords. Having a weapon in my hand is terribly frightful. I'm weak. Wrestling anyone else my age would result in me having a sore behind and broken bones. The other two will never happen. When I turn sixteen, my father is going to throw me into the Royal Guard. He grew up a soldier, so I must follow his footsteps. Pitiful really. I'm sure the only reason he wants me to follow his footsteps is to make me feel the same pain he felt when mother died. It's vengeance, not love, that sets his eyes on creating a soldier out of me. I'm a skinny runt. I will die my first day at war.

Resting my feet on the branch and propping my back against the trunk, I watch city-square bustle with people. The townspeople, a quiet reserved sort, tend to mind their own business, that is if no one discusses money or King Oscar. Both of those are sore subjects. Not like anybody can really protest against a monarchy. Feudalism was the inventor of necessary submission. Being born to a high ranking general, I should have a promising future in this bleak societal system. But the opposite remains true. The Manor, where my father lives, is full of stuck-up, spoiled rotten kids that stick their noses up at any passing plebian. I can't fit in with those sorts of people. I'd much rather interact with those that struggle to survive than those that live luxuriously. Whenever I get the chance, I run off for that purpose — to be with those I best relate with.

Looking at the main entrance to city-square, I spot a beaten horse. Its head hangs low and noticeable scars mark its snout, but it's the rider on the open carriage that is interesting. He's seemingly unconscious. Shouting, the guards from the watch towers above call out at the man to stop, but his horse continues to move forward. Through the leaves I am sitting behind, I can't make out the rider's face, but his side is bulging out and his body bows like a tree on a windy day. Pulling up beside the box of sticks drawn by a wounded black horse, a guard grabs hold of the leather reins attached to the bit in the horse's mouth. Coming to a halt, the horse sways side to side.

"Wheel this man over to the doc!" shouts the guard clothed in brown leather armor.

Jumping from the branch onto the grass below, I walk out to the side of the cobblestone road, one of four which lead to the center of the city. Stretching my neck so I can see better, I see that the rider is clothed in torn sackcloth. His eyes are shut and blood leaks from the corner of his mouth. Racing out by the side of the carriage is another guard with a wagon to carry the unconscious rider. Lifting him gently into the sturdy wagon, the two guards draw the attention of many nearby townspeople who peek out their townhouse windows or doors. The people roving the stores scatter out of the way. The guard who brought out the wagon gallops off towards Doctor Commons, spitting up stones behind his wheels. Tearing away from my resting spot, I bolt through the city streets, weaving in and out of the lanes and running by the stone houses. Doctor Commons isn't far from where I am; the guard will only beat me there by a small margin of time. Not far from The Manor, Doctor Commons practices medicine in a double story stone brick office. Most of his living quarters are upstairs, but his office is

2

on the ground floor. Panting, I can see his place down the street. The guard's wagon is out front, empty. Running inside, I see the rider sprawled across Doctor Commons' leather cushioned bed for patients. The narrow-faced guard marches past me with a shove as he heads out for his horse. Doctor Commons reaches into a glass door medicine cabinet for what looks like white gauzes.

Stepping closer, I say, "Hey, Doc."

Doctor Commons pulls out a couple gauzes, raises his bottle-like spectacles, and looks at me. A smile replaces his sober face as he replies, "Hey, Tommy."

Glancing at the rider in sackcloth, I ask, "Who's the old man?"

Rubbing his wispy white hair, Doctor Commons shrugs, "Don't know. Neither do the weasels. The one who dropped this fellow off gave me no salutation and just demanded I help him. He said, 'I know nothing about this blasted intruder.' What stiff-necked pinheads."

Most people refer to the guards and soldiers as weasels it has been a well-accepted title, but not by the soldiers themselves.

Groaning, the rider who looks like an aged monk cracks open his eyes.

"It's coming," he moans, writhing his body to his right.

Hurrying to his side, I press my hand against his arm so that he stops moving.

"It's coming," he moans louder.

"What is?" I ask, holding the man still.

"It's coming," he moans even louder before slipping back into unconsciousness.

Doctor Commons walks over and presses the gauzes against the cut on the side of his mouth soaking up the blood.

"What do you suppose he meant?" I ask.

Doctor Commons merely shrugs and says, "Some fantasy of his, I suppose. Nothing to worry about. He looks like he took a mighty blow to the head, though. He got a goose egg as round as my elbow above the nape of his neck."

Stepping behind the man, I kneel so I can see what Doctor Commons is talking about. Protruding from the back of the man's long gray hair is a giant bump parting it. "He got a goose egg all right. More like a mountain, actually."

Doctor Commons douses a white cloth with a clear liquid and applies the cloth gently to the back of the man's head. "There's not much to do with that, but I see an open cut at its peak. Cleansing it a bit may prevent an onset of infection."

Dabbing the black and blue bump, Doctor Commons tells me to bring him a bandage for a wound at the top of the man's shoulder. There is a tear there like he was attacked by a hungry bear. Finding the wrap bandages beneath a small bottle of mercury, I rush back over, and apply the adhesive given to me by Doctor Commons to keep the end down. Putting the beige bandages away, I notice a golden ring on the man's portly left hand. Not where a typical wedding ring goes, but rather on the middle finger. A pesky shadow rests atop the golden ring due to the oil lamp hanging above the bench. Easing forward, I raise the man's ring to my face. Engraved in it is the word "truth." Letting his hand swing down by his side, I observe the rest of his clothing. Nothing but bloody, torn rags cover him. His ring stands out as an anomaly compared to the rest of him.

"Tommy, stop eyeing that stranger with such fascination. Give him some space. You look like a vulture preying on a dead carcass," Doctor Commons says with a light chuckle, "Nothing like your father, you are."

"No one is like my father. Who just a week after their first-born's arrival rides to some foreign land for a month stay? Who in this bloody city does that? No one, but my father," I scoff, stepping back from the beaten man.

Sighing, Doctor Commons replies, "Your father had and still has a lot on his plate. I know his seeming indifference—"

"Callousness!"

"Fine, callousness, is hard to handle. However, he was taught to be hard. He is a general after all. Fortifying fortresses, defending the city, and leading brigades is what he does. Europe is an ever expanding and ever developing place. Your father understands that and wages war accordingly."

"To leave his son sitting at his bedroom window just wondering when he will return."

"Many times, my window. You are able to stay tonight as well if your father won't be home."

"I doubt he will. The king called upon him this morning."

"Then you may find refuge here for the night. You know where the bed is."

Nodding, I kick a white pebble across the oak floor. "It's coming!"

Turning around, I spot the rider grappling the sides of the bed so hard that his knuckles are as white as ghosts. Jolting his whole body like a possessed man, he rocks back and forth screaming the same phrase, "It's coming! It's coming!" Then after a few seconds, he relaxes again, falling back to sleep.

Staring at Doctor Commons, I see his face crease with wrinkles that weren't there before. "More fantasies?" I ask.

"I suppose. Don't know much about this lad. I suppose he will come to eventually. At that moment, we can answer some questions. I guess we shall wait till he is more aware of himself," Doctor Commons sighs, sitting down on his wooden stool.

Wandering around searching for the other gnarly stool, I ask, "What do you think he is? A monk? I think he is a monk. Or maybe some crazed sot who had too much mead." I laugh as I sit on the other stool I found beneath his desk.

Shaking his head, Doctor Commons replies, "I doubt he's a drunk. His breath is much too clear for that. A monk? Maybe. But what monk comes to the city? Or what monk has such scraggly gray hair? I'd say he is some roving traveler with no place to call home. A pitiful state I must say, but to each his own."

"Why he is as dry as a desert. Where you think his money pouch would be? Not a sight of gold on him besides his peculiar ring."

Shrugging, Doctor Commons sighs, "I have no clue. Maybe he was robbed. You know those dirt roads are no place for the weak in heart."

"Glad I'm going to be in the Royal Guard," I scoff.

Nodding, Doctor Commons scratches at his face replying, "Yes in forty days you will be sixteen. Your father will waste no time sending you off with the Royal Guard. Soon enough you'll have beady eyes and a conniving black nose." He was trying to make me feel better, but his joke was only enough to extract a grunt from me. "It won't be that bad, Tommy."

"I'll be out on the dirt roads with thieves and beggars. I'll be parading around in armor while dueling with some other fellow who will probably slice and dice me like a legume. Worst of all, I'll be forced to slave away in the barracks. I hate 'The Guard;' it deserves no 'royal' title."

"Your father—"

"My father was an ox at my age. He was fine. I on the other hand look like a starved mule. Look at my ribs," I say, untucking my shirt which my father bought for me ever since royalty was expected to have a pair of what they call trousers and a ruffled top. Lifting it, I show Doctor Commons my skeleton body.

Frowning, Doctor Commons waves his hand in the air like a school master saying, "Put your shirt back down. I pray that you don't do that in public."

"I would never. I am no male strumpet who cavorts wantonly playing my sex like some trumpet," I say with a mischievous smirk as I tuck my white-collar shirt back in.

"In my right mind I'd wash your mouth clean with soap, but I'm much too soft."

"Yes, you are far too kind," I laugh.

Smiling at me, Doctor Commons replies, "That means you're lucky," looking back at the sleeping rider Doctor Commons continues on, "He may sleep the rest of his days at this rate. The sun will soon fall beneath the earth in a couple hours. I'm going to wash up and boil some water to make stew. I suppose you want dinner as well."

"Oh, yes. A strumpet must eat every meal to keep gold in his pouch. A full figure appears much better."

"Enough of that. Harlotry is no joke. As a man, you know that. Now, let me see what I can find."

After spending the next few hours chatting, making stew, and eating, I found it no trouble to fall asleep peacefully with a full stomach.

Chapter 2

Shaking me awake, Doctor Commons shouts, "Wake, Tommy! Wake!"

Cracking my heavy eyelids open, I ask, "What is it, Doc?"

"Do you know of the rider's whereabouts?"

"Down in your office," I sigh, closing my eyes again.

Jostling me like a sack of potatoes, Doctor Commons shakes his head violently. "No! He is no longer there!"

Fighting the urge to go back to sleep again, I inquire, "Did he go for a pee? The ditch is right outside you know."

"No. Of course I checked that first."

"You tried to walk in on a man peeing?"

"Stop this fooling around! Help me look for him!"

"Why?"

"I can't find my mercury!"

Sitting up, I shake out all the butterflies in my head and ask, "What need would he have for mercury?"

"That is what worries me. I have not the slightest idea, but I know that element is terribly expensive and not easy to come by."

Prying myself away from my bed, I slip into my cloak and follow Doctor Commons who is already hurrying down the steps.

"We need to find him. I must have my mercury back," Doctor Commons says slurring his words together.

Waving his frazzled hair, he throws on his black suit coat over his nightgown.

Looking at me, he notices my amusement at his insistence on dressing respectable and says, "Despite this great calamity, I will not forget who I am."

Opening the door, Doctor Commons welcomes a flood of blinding sunlight to surround us. Tugging at his suit coat and flattening his hair with his other hand, he marches outside speedily. I trail behind him in a much less dignified manner. Even if his life was on the line, he would take the time to dress properly if it meant he had to go outside. He says at the University of Cambridge they demand professionalism, especially from medical doctors. I could never be a doctor then.

"Hurry now, don't dawdle," Doctor Commons scolds me as I yawn for the whole world to hear.

"Where do you think that fellow would be? Not like a blasted traveler will find company among city folks. Like you said, thieves fill these parts," I say, watching my feet scuffle against the cobblestone.

"Enough of that. The world has too many pessimists as it is. It's time man changes his perspective on things."

"Or maybe you're just stubborn like an ass with a grudge against his owner."

"Hush now, Tommy. None of that. You respect your elders. You hear?"

"Yeah, Doc." Heading towards the city-square, I notice a crowd of townspeople huddling close to the execution square. "Is there an execution today?"

"No. Not that I am aware of," Doctor Commons replies, looking down at his golden pocket watch given to him on the day of his graduation from the University of Cambridge.

"Then how come there is a flock of people eyeing The Square?"

Looking up from his pocket watch drawn across his suit coat by a golden chain, he squints his eyes.

Rounding the corner of the last townhouse, we come into the city-square.

"Saint Moses," Doctor Commons gasps, eyeing with wonder at The Square.

In front of the gallows that loom over the center of the city is the rider still in his sackcloth suit, delivering a message to the people with great ferocity in his display.

Waving around in his hand the bottle of mercury, he shouts with great vigor, "Your fate will surely come! Just as sure as death would find me if I took just one sip of this virulent poison!"

"That blasted hooligan is making a mockery out of himself," Doctor Commons huffs. "What time is it that such a fool would prate like a tippler from a tavern?" As he looks down at his watch, the church bell rings out across the city twelve times as it does at midday as well as midnight.

"I suppose that answers your question, Doc," I say, stepping out beside him. Caught up in his trying-to-still-look-professional rage, Doctor Commons begins to march up towards The Square with a full head of steam, but the dense crowd does not permit him to go much farther.

"From the day of my arrival you had forty days left before your utter destruction, but now that day has past, and your fate will be in the hands of The Beast in a thirty-nine-day period!" proclaims the rider like a prophet.

"Aye. You have been tipping a couple back my friend," mocks a random man from the crowd. I cannot see him from where I am at, but his voice is haggardly like he is a heavy smoker.

"Too many days spent at the madhouse I presume," another man comments with the approval of the crowd as they laugh.

Crushing his fat neck with his plump chin, the rider bows his neck with shame, but still is able to utter, "I know it sounds outrageous, but you must believe me. I have seen it myself."

"The Beast? You seen The Beast? Was it when you looked in the mirror, you fool?" scoffs a middle-aged woman with gray hair, her children dance around her like clowns.

"No, The Beast is fierce with a golden crown around his horned head and many bared teeth at his disposal," the rider retorts, still frantically waving his arms around, nearly sending the bottle of mercury across the cobblestone road.

"Now hold up there, mister! That is my fine mercury you're jostling around! I demand you give it back, whoever you are!" Doctor Commons shouts, waving his gloved fist in the air.

The rider stares at Doctor Commons like he never saw such a sight before, and he probably hasn't. Not many see a man in his nightgown in the middle of the day. Especially one who tries to cover it up by wearing a suit coat. "My name is Jonah, actually. Who are you?" the rider replies, leaning his ear towards Doctor Commons.

"I am the man who attended to your blasted head, you strutting peacock. Now if I don't get my mercury back, I may reverse the good I had done and clobber you over the head!" Doctor Commons squawks, pushing his way through the crowd which watches the spectacle with amusement.

Looking at the bottle of mercury, Jonah shakes his head, saying, "You want this toxin? Why, it does no good except killing those who no longer find the desire to live."

"That is top of the line mercury which is a medical delicacy and is acclaimed by the University of Cambridge as the most essential medicine. Now if you don't mind, I'd like to have it back, dear sir," Doctor Commons argues as he finally reaches the front of the crowd with his palm out stretched for the bottle.

Shrugging his shoulders indifferently, Jonah hands Doctor Commons his bottle of mercury. "There you go, sir. I still don't see why you find that dastardly thing so valuable."

"Maybe if you were educated, you would understand. You blasted hooligan." Marching his way back towards me, Doctor Commons refuses to look back at Jonah. And Jonah doesn't seem to mind as he goes back to spewing out his ridiculous prophecies.

"The Beast may even be among you as we speak," he says, "clawing at your infrastructure right now." Clawing the air like a lion, Jonah hisses.

"He's madder than a hatter!" cries a young dame with beautiful black hair.

"A middle-aged virgin, undoubtedly!" cries a rugged man clothed with an apron only a blacksmith wears, "Looks like he can't even afford a strumpet either. A blasted celibate with not an ounce of gold to his name."

"This is no way to treat yourselves before your definite end!" Jonah shouts back.

"Go to hell, you lunatic!" shouts the dame with beautiful black hair.

"Yeah! You mad celibate!" cries the blacksmith.

"Listen!" shouts Jonah, but in vain. The whole crowd is screaming, chucking fruits, clothes, and baskets at him without a care.

"He'll be tarred and feathered at this rate," Doctor Commons grunts, slipping his bottle of mercury into his coat pocket.

"I feel kind of bad for the fellow," I say, biting my bottom lip.

"Why?"

"Well, he may be mad, but that gives the people no reason to make a mockery out of him. He's like a child sharing his fantasies. He may be confused, but he is presenting no harm," I say, watching Jonah walk shamefully away from The Square as an assortment of melons, squashes, and green beans fly by his head and some up against his curved back. The townspeople have never liked hearing about change; whenever they have heard about change, it was King Oscar raising the cost of living.

13

Hanging his head like there are shackles around his neck, Jonah leaves behind the mocking crowd calling out several nasty names.

"Yeah! Run you hunchback!"

"Loony!"

"Jabber!"

"Leave, clown!"

"Vestal Virgin!"

So many people are shouting I no longer know who is saying what.

"Leave them to their devices. A small tumult calls for no worry, but revolution is what you must beware," Doctor Commons grumbles, turning back towards his office.

Behind us are a troupe of soldiers dressed in common leather armor banded across their chests. Their hands are set upon the hilts of their swords as they stare at us with glacier cold eyes.

"What is the cause of such an uproar?" the middle guard asks with a voice that reminds me of a bear growling. His stature is tall and built strong.

"A lunatic has prophesied the end of our kingdom. He has merely been chased off The Square," Doctor Commons replies.

"What end?"

"Something about a beast."

"Fool." The guards ease their hands from their swords. "We will summon this crowd back to business. Excuse us." Marching in between Doctor Commons and I, the guards wave their arms around shouting, "Show's over!"

Dispersing calmly without complaint, the crowd goes back to their earlier business whether it be selling crops, hauling works of metal, or just doing plain old errands.

"That loon is a blasted trouble maker already," Doctor Commons mumbles, walking back to his office. I trail behind, but I'm unable to keep myself from looking

14

back on occasion at The Square. The gloomy gallows still sit there empty, sending a strange chill down my back. A sensation of nervous energy. A strange omen.

Chapter 3

The church bell summons the arrival of midnight, but I am not asleep. Gazing out the window by Doctor Commons' guest room bed, I wait for my father. I got word from a friend of mine earlier in the day that my father was sent out by the king to collect taxes from some of the farmers outside The North Wall and was returning tonight. I may try to convince myself that I feel indifferent towards my father, but I do not. I very much resent him for all the burdens he casts upon me along with the maltreatment he uses against me to get his way, but deep inside I desire a relationship with him just as much as any boy does with his father. Granted, it may be my fault that our relationship has never been healthy. I hardly ever sleep at The Manor where all the nobles live because I simply can't. Either my father is not there, or when he is, he beats me, yells at me, or at the very least ignores me. It's rather unpleasant to be under the same roof as a cold-hearted monster. Yet, I was born because of that monster, and in a way I'm still a part of him.

So, I sit by the window, waiting. Waiting for my father to march by with his regiment behind him, but all I see are owls roosting beside our neighbor's chimney. Stiller then a puddle of muddy water, I sit. My concentration is entirely directed at the cobblestone path that bypasses my window. I wait anxiously, knowing all so well that he will probably never actually come by. He never was a man of his word.

On the verge of slipping into dreamer's paradise, I hear the stamping of hooves against the stones. Perking my ears, I sit up on my knees hoping to see my father. For what reason? That I don't even know. The first person to enter my sights is a royal guard dressed in his fine gold-plated armor. He looks like a lieutenant lavished with medals across his chest. Following him is another similarly dressed Royal Guard member. Then riding in on a horse is my father, bearing his ocean blue sapphire armor decked out with polished golden medals, a shield made of ivory, and a sword made from precious stones. These men definitely aren't returning from a day of collecting taxes but rather from a splendid party, or maybe they are heading towards one. The king is known to throw many parties for those of great prestige at the expense of his people. Marching behind my father are two more royal guards who soon pass by as well. Sitting by my window, I once again am left watching the owls atop my neighbor's roof. Yawning, I feel the onset of sleep catch hold of me. I have seen my father. That's what I wanted, or so I tell myself. It's sad my goal is only to see my father and not to actually know him. Searching for my pillow like a blind man, I pat my bed several times till my fingers graze the end of my feather pillow.

Tucking myself back into bed, I close my eyes, but it isn't long till murmurs wake me. Rising again to my knees, I peek out the window. Two men are pulling a wagon covered with a large bear skin stop. They set the wagon down. Dressed in filthy rags, they take swigs from what I can tell are small glass bottles. After drinking, the shortest of the two asks, "What that fellow tell ya'?"

Shrugging, the taller man says, "Fellow didn't say much. Just said the man hanged self. Bury him. He no honor."

"Poor fellow. Suppose he reason for his doing?"

"No mead for his lips, I guess," the taller man jokes, chugging the last of his drink.

"Or a wife who nagged the poor fellow," the shorter man jests, also finishing his drink.

"So, we take this fellow to The Pit?"

"Suppose. Bury him with the other bastards."

"'Less we feed 'im to the buzzards."

"Might have hung himself, but he no dog."

"That they do with heads of Square victims."

"He ain't no Square victim."

"Died like one."

"Blasted bonehead, don't you see he ain't no criminal. Criminals are bungled in the head, they need to be rotted out."

"Aye, whatever. Let's just get this over with. I got an empty bottle and need a fill."

Grabbing the wagon again, the two men pull it away following the same path my father took. *Who could they be?* Slipping out of bed, I sneak down the stairs by Doctor Commons' room out onto the rough cobblestone street. Curiosity has always been one of my downfalls. Creeping through the darkness, I find the two drunks meandering their way to the edge of the city where The Pit is located. Staggering forward, the two men finally reach The Pit setting the wagon down.

"Why you wonder that fellow hadn't lend us his horse?" asks the taller man.

"He ain't just a fellow. He some high sort. Something important I reckon he went to," the shorter man replies.

"Blasted weasel wasn't toting nothing but himself."

"You bonehead, he was no weasel. No weasel wears that shiny stuff."

"'Less he the commander of something."

"Shut your trap you blasted fool, and help me bury this poor fellow."

Reaching into the wagon, they pull out two shovels and begin to work away at the stony soil. Stalking closer, I crouch directly behind the wagon. A terrible smell of rotting flesh burns my nostrils as flies go to and fro around the bear skin. Peeking around the corner of the wagon, I check to see if the two drunks are going to come back over, but they're too busy arguing with each other about where to start digging. Lifting the edge of the bear skin while pinching my nose shut, I give open space for an army of flies to swarm my face. Shutting my mouth and keeping my nose pinched, I don't let any of the flies get inside my body. As soon as the flies disperse themselves, I open my eyes. A head belonging to some sort of white-haired farmer stares back at me. His eye sockets are a home for hundreds of maggots who crawl all over each other. Swallowing a large lump of saliva, I cover my mouth with my quivering hand.

Who is that?

Finding the strength to take another look, I examine the maggot head. Around his neck is a circle of discolored skin that's more purple than a mistress's finest lavender that she dips in before meeting with her lover.

This man did hang himself.

A golden earring sticks through his ear. It is a simple ring of gold. This is the keeper of the farmers. Often referred to as just keeper. He is the representative who speaks for the farmers before the Royal Union who are the ones who help run the city beside the king. King Oscar gave the farmers a representative to negate their ideas of revolution, but in reality, the keeper means little to the Royal Union. He is basically a glorified farmer with a monthly wage given to him by the king as long as he attends their meetings. Sure, in front of the public King Oscar will dutifully praise the keeper, but in private the king will treat the keeper as any other farmer.

"Aye, I believe this ditch fits him well," says the tall drunk stumbling towards the wagon. Crawling away through the long grass, I scamper back into the cobblestone city. The two men were too intoxicated to notice me. Walking back to Doctor Commons' place, I tip toe inside and back up to my bed. Tucking myself in again, I promise myself I will figure out why the keeper killed himself, especially knowing all so well that suicide means he is deprived of an honorable funeral. Then again, no funeral is very honorable unless you are of great prestige. He was the keeper, but he is only a step higher than an average farmer who are about as low as they come.

Yet why would he kill himself?

Chapter 4

"Go back to your tavern, tipper!" the same blacksmith from yesterday shouts.

Jonah stands at The Square again wearing the same clothes he had on yesterday, preaching the same message with more details. The crowd still finds no room for Jonah in their hearts, but rather are even louder than yesterday.

"Aye, how many times will it take me to say this? Go back to your wormhole!" an elderly gentleman shouts, raising a wrinkly fist in the air.

"Please understand. I do not jest you when I speak these horrible prophecies," Jonah insists, "I speak with truth on my lips—"

"There's more than truth on those lips. More like fresh ale!" someone else hollers.

"I agree!" affirms the blacksmith.

"The Beast will not be kind. He works in the darkness. He haunts dreams," Jonah continues.

"You haunt my midday. I come out here to grab me some meat and you're up there spreading lies. I can't get a thing," a gray-haired woman gripes with a basket in the crook of her arm.

The crowd has somehow taken over most of the city-square. I stand where Doctor Commons and I stood last time Jonah was talking nonsense.

"He may drive some to think of the terrible. Whether it be murder or stealing or—" Jonah says as he's interrupted.

"Where's my husband!? Where in this blasted cold-hearted city is my husband!?" cries a homely woman dressed in a plain linen gown. Her feet are bare, and her hair is mangled like she just got out of bed. "Where is he!? Where is he!? Where!?" Tearing at her hair, she begins to bawl. Tears run all over her beet red face.

"Lady what seems to be the issue?" Jonah asks from The Square.

Glaring at Jonah, she cries, "You ass! My husband is missing! That's what's wrong!" Balling up her fists, she waves them around, angrier than a wet cat.

Walking about keeping an eye on the crowd, a common guard of the gate notices the weeping woman.

Marching up to her, he leans in towards her with his hands behind his back asking, "What is the problem, madam?"

Socking him right in the mouth, the lady retorts, "My husband is missing, you weasel!"

Moving his hands by his side while shifting his jaw back and forth, the guard struggles within himself to keep a cool demeanor. "I'm sorry, madam. If I may take you to my chief, he may be able to help."

"Would he know where he is?"

"Only one way to find out, madam."

"Stop calling me that. Just take me there."

"Yes, right this way." Pointing down towards the Gate House where the common guards typically bunk, he leads her down towards his chief.

A terrible pity falls on me for the woman. Running up behind the two, I whisper, "I may know where he is."

Turning around quicker than a war horse, the lady asks with wide eyes, "Where?"

"Is he the keeper?"

"Yes!"

"I'm afraid I saw him last night being buried in The Pit."

In shock the lady is unable to scream, cry, or move. She stands there frozen with her mouth hanging down to her breasts. "Take me there," she whispers.

"But—" the guard stutters.

"Take me there, you wretched fool!" the lady shrieks, punching the guard several times in his gut until he finally submits with a look of fear in his dark brown eyes.

"OK, let's go," the tall and lanky guard whispers, "Where did you see him buried in The Pit, boy?"

"I'll show you," I say.

Not wasting a step, the sorrowful farm lady bounds towards The Pit with crimson cheeks continuing to be washed over with fresh tears. Reaching The Pit, which is practically a mound of dirt, she falls onto her knees clawing away at the soil.

Pulling her to her feet, the guard turns towards me saying, "Now where was he buried?"

Scanning The Pit, I notice an empty bottle.

"There," I say pointing where the bottle sits.

Jumping out of the guard's arms, the lady tears at the dirt.

Not even trying to stop her the guard looks towards me saying, "Find a shovel."

Nodding, I run off for Doctor Commons' office. In his shed out back, he has many tools, a shovel being one of them. Quickly throwing aside his working gloves, saw, and shears, I find his wooden handled shovel with an iron head. Hurrying back to The Pit, I see that the lady is still burrowing a hole after her lost husband. Handing the shovel to the guard, I watch him reluctantly take it and begin to shovel across from the troubled lady. He makes certain that he doesn't get any closer to her than he must, like she has the plague or something.

Heaving away mounds of stony soil, the guard asks, "Are you sure he's here?"

I nod, replying, "Yes."

"I haven't come across him yet."

25

"I don't know how far they dug."

"Who's 'they'?"

"I don't know who the fellows were."

Staring at me with his eyebrows knitted together, the guard shakes his head and continues to work at the dirt.

"Was he in a coffin?" the guard asks.

I shake my head.

"He was not."

"Stop blabbering. Just get him out," the troubled lady says in between sobs.

A strange thud sounds from the guard's shovel. A sickening thud.

"I believe I struck an arm," he says.

Leaping into the freshly dug hole, the keeper's wife lets out a shrill cry.

"Get him out!" she shrieks.

Pushing her aside gently, the guard brushes away the dirt from the keeper's upper body till he finds where his face is. It's him with his maggot sockets.

Instantly, the keeper's wife lays herself out on top of her dead husband, crying, "It's him! It's him!"

Looking up at me from his knees, the guard asks sternly, "How'd you know he was buried?"

"I saw the two men who buried him go by my window. I snuck out behind them to see what they were doing toting such a large wagon around," I say. I must sound foolish. Everyone knows never to follow someone at night. It only means a couple things. Either they are meeting a woman, the sort no holy man would visit, or they are performing discrete business. The kind that may get someone wound up in The Pit.

"Two men? What were they like?" the guard asks.

"Simple folks. Not very educated and not very sober."

"What'd they look like?"

"Can't say. It was dark outside."

"This was done at night?"

26

"Yes. They said something about him hanging himself."

Scanning the dead body, the guard nods his head saying, "Looks like he did."

"He would never," the keeper's wife wails from her prostrate position.

"Maybe the two men you speak of hanged him," the guard says.

I shake my head saying, "I doubt they could find their way around the farms in their condition much less kill someone."

"Well, fetch me my chief. I must speak to him. He'll be in the nearest room to your right inside the Gate House. Tell him Jonathan sent you."

Nodding, I bolt towards the Gate House. The large crowd at city-square has broken into small groups whispering among themselves. Jonah must have left. Bulging from the wall beside the main gate is a rectangular office which happens to be the Gate House. Bursting inside without a proper knock, I am quickly apprehended by two guards who are standing by the door.

"Unhand me, I was sent by Jonathan!" I exclaim.

Raising my feet off the ground, the two guards simply laugh. Their strong arms hardly flex to lift me up, then again I am lighter than a bird.

"Nice try, you pesky little rat," the guard on my right says jostling me around.

"I'm serious," I snap back.

"Sure, you are as serious as a joker who clowns at the tavern."

Kicking and squirming, I try my best to get out of their grasps. Looking over to where Jonathan said his chief would be, I spot him looking down at some letters written with black ink. He doesn't bother to look up at the skirmish right in front of his desk. His eyes are swimming in the ink before him. Each letter grabs his attention. They must be important.

"I am here for Jonathan's chief," I say, hoping to grab the chief's attention, but he still doesn't give me a glance. He is an older gentleman with thin white hair and a face that reminds me of a grumpy dragon.

"Why would he tell you to do that?" the guard on my left asks.

"The keeper was hanged," I say bluntly. Looking up slowly from his letter, the chief sets it down, pushing it aside.

"Put him down," he says with a voice that should only belong to a sore throat frog.

"Chief—"

"Do as you're told soldier."

"Yes, Chief," the guard on the right complies as he and his partner set me down on my feet. Standing up straight, Jonathan's chief approaches me in his leather tunic with an iron breastplate across his chest.

Eyeing me up, the chief cracks a small crooked smile asking, "Aren't you the son of the most respectable General Damon?"

"Yes."

"You have his eyes."

Hiding my disgust, I reply, "Thank you, sir. However, I am here because of Jonathan."

"Yes, you said something about Keeper Peppers being hanged?"

"I suppose, if that's his name."

"It is. What makes you fancy this notion?"

"His body is in The Pit, sir. Jonathan has called upon you because the keeper's wife is up there weeping something awful."

"I see," says the chief, "I guess I should see this matter through then. Come with me, son of Damon." Marching outside, the chief gestures for me to follow him. The two guards who apprehended me earlier glare at me suspiciously as I walk by them. Taking his time, the chief is in no rush to reach The Pit. He simply meanders up the slight incline like he is taking a Sunday stroll. Half of his steps seem to go more to the side rather than forward. It irritates me, but I refrain from speaking. He is a chief after all.

By the time we reach The Pit Jonathan runs our way. The keeper's wife is still crying over her husband, not letting him go.

"Chief, glad you could make it. It seems that the keeper has hung himself and was buried last night by two drunks."

"Jonathan, slow down. Now, how do you know all this?"

Glancing over at me, he points, saying, "He told me mostly, sir. However, the corpse's neck does look like it was hanging upon some rope for quite a while."

"That is not just any corpse. That is my husband you're talking about," the keeper's wife wails, digging her fingers into her dead husband's chest.

Ignoring her, the chief continues to speak with Jonathan, "I see." Looking at me, the chief asks, "How did you know about all this."

"I saw it from my window, and I followed the two men who buried him."

"Why would you do something so foolish?"

"Curiosity, I guess."

Observing the situation, the chief finally shrugs, saying, "Not much can be done about it now. If the poor fellow hung himself and was buried by strangers, what am I or anyone to do? Just leave it be." His reply was quick. Too quick. Almost as if he didn't plan on resolving the issue when he came up here. Like he simply wanted to make sure what he heard was true.

"You lazy ass! You lazy no for good weasel! My husband is dead! He would never kill himself! Never!" the keeper's wife shrieks, diving out of her husband's grave and after the chief who just watches, amused. Before she can reach him, Jonathan usurps her keeping her back. "I'll kill you! I'll kill all of you damned weasels!"

29

"Now I understand this is hard to accept, madam. However, your husband is dead and there is nothing that we can do," the chief says coldly, walking back towards the Gate House.

"I'll kill you! I'll kill you damn weasel! You hear me? You hear?! I'll kill you!"

The fire in her eyes and the ghost white paleness around her balled up fists don't simply express her rage, but promise the chief's death. They guarantee it. She is going to kill him somehow, somewhere, sometime.

Chapter 5

Waking to another day in Doctor Commons' bed, I dress myself in a simple tunic of mine before heading out for the city-square. For some odd reason I had a notion to see Jonah again speak atop The Square. Arriving earlier than normal, I notice that Jonah is not yet there. So, to pass the time I snoop around town munching on an apple for breakfast. Everyone who walks by is chattering among themselves whether it be in pairs or groups. I pick up on bits of pieces from those around me and the topic most are talking about focuses around Jonah and his odd prophecies. However, some spoke about the Keeper and his strange death. Nothing quite this interesting has occurred here before. The common folk tend to live rather unmeaningful lives. They are born to pay taxes, eat, sleep in their small homes, and die. It's a rather depressing life surrounded by gray cobblestone and empty chatter that avoids all the serious topics everyone keeps hidden to themselves.

Striking twelve times, the church bell summons midday and as it does, I spot Jonah rising onto The Square beneath the looming gallows that casts a shadow across his round face.

"Afternoon again my friends!" he acclaims trying to get everyone's attention. Without another word the people flock his way like sheep to still waters. "I see you all seem very anxious today."

"What you have to say about yesterday?" someone asks from the already large crowd.

"What about yesterday?" Jonah replies.

"The Keeper's apparent suicide."

"I see. I'd say it is a work of the enemy."

"The Beast?"

"Yes, he works in the night."

"That was when he was buried," a young-looking man says with flour across his black apron.

"How do you know?" asks the young dame with beautiful black hair.

"I heard that from my brother he works as a guard."

"A weasel told me such things as well," says the blacksmith.

"Aye, me too," another man says.

"Do not doubt that this will be the first and only incident," Jonah says waving his finger in the air, "there will be more."

"How are we to know this isn't some coincidence?" the blacksmith asks, "Any fellow could kill himself. Ain't no reason to get ruffled."

"He is right," the dame with beautiful black hair says.

"I tell you this is what he wants. To divide you people apart. He will do this anyway he can. He'll give you nightmares, he'll kill, he'll do anything."

"I thought you said he'll come in forty days. Not now," objects the baker with flour on his apron.

"Yes, his physical form won't arrive till then, but his spirit is already here."

"What are we to do about that?" asks the dame with beautiful black hair.

"Don't be rash but be calm. Keep a straight mind and seek after wisdom. Nothing he does can harm you if you don't jump into his logical fallacies."

"You still talk foolishly, my friend," says the baker shaking his head, "I can't see how any of this can be true. You're still just a loon."

"Aye, he is," says another after another till the crowd is nothing, but a scarce handful of people. Most of which are drunks who only make enough to buy cheap beer from the local tavern. Stepping closer, I prepare to listen in on what they are discussing, but a stern hand catches me by the shoulder spinning me around. Standing tall with his royal apparel on, my father glares at me like an angry wolf.

Tightening the belt to his baggy golden trimmed trousers, he says "What is this that I hear? Have you gone mad?" His voice is so distinctive and very guttural. It reminds me of an ailing bear. It fits him well since he has the build of a giant grizzly.

"What do you mean?" I ask.

"Sir. What do you mean, sir?"

"What do you mean, sir?"

"That's better. I am speaking of yesterday. The chief of the Gate House told me you snuck out one night to find the Keeper being buried."

I simply nod.

"Why? Why would you be so foolish. Now you have caused a great disturbance to fall upon so many. This matter could have been made less a plight if you didn't go on about what you saw."

"I hardly spoke of it."

Latching hold of my shoulders, he shakes me violently bellowing, "Don't lie to me! I heard you have been spreading rumors according to Chief Myles."

Stepping back with a huff, I reply, "I said I did not. You believe Myles over me?"

"I'll believe a jester over you. Now come with me."

"To where?"

"You're coming with me to The Manor."

"Why?"

Grabbing me by the arm, he drags me behind him saying, "Don't argue with me."

The Manor, the overly luxurious, overly beautiful place all the rich pricks live that take advantage of their people. I have a room in my father's abode, but I only sleep there on occasions that I cannot be with Doctor Commons. It has a far nicer bed complete with satin sheets, wool comforters, and a silky pillow filled with the finest feathers, but I'd rather feel secure in Doctor Commons' abode then find myself feeling alone inside The Manor where no one understands me. All the children who live there and all those my age are upright brats with not a sense of humility inside them. Entering through two ivory gates that lead into a winsome grove, my father continues to drag me along the marble path that only can be found in The Manor. Reaching the end of the grove complete with the most beautiful flowering trees, my father opens the towering doors that lead into The Manor made of the finest stones, marble, and even some gold and silver to give the mansion a polished look. Our city exports many goods gaining much wealth from doing so. However only those at the top truly relish the prosperity of our city. Every month a wagon of precious stones rides into The Manor through the entrance outback big enough for carriages. That's where King Oscar normally enters.

Once my father and I are inside The Manor itself he lets me go and urges me along professionally with his hands back and his head upright. With great honor comes great image and my father would never want his image to be defiled. Marching through the velvet hallways, we reach an overarching portal made of precious stones that has no door, but rather is open to the garden in the center of The Manor. Placed symmetrical with each other, the luxurious homes made for people like my father are amidst the beautiful garden always budding with fresh flowers. Their bases are made of snowbird marble, but their walls are made of well sanded and polished stones complete with flat roofs that have only one chimney. Heading towards the nearest house to our right, we enter through the golden trimmed door into my father's abode. Inside at the cherry table is Chief Myles in the center of my father's kitchen. At my arrival he rises to his feet dressed in what he wore last time I saw him except he also has on his many badges of honor on his right shoulder. Those at The Manor love prestige more than wealth even.

Setting his cold black eyes on mine, he says with a grin, "I have been waiting to talk with you."

Looking up at my father, I ask, "Why is he here?"

"He needed to expel some knowledge upon you and you better listen or I will take the switch to you."

"Take a seat," Chief Myles says, pulling out one of my father's cherry wood chairs. Sitting down, I sweat heavily feeling the ring of perspiration around the neck of my tunic.

"I'll be up in my chamber, Chief Myles. Speak to my son as you will. Don't be afraid to speak harshly if necessary," my father says, walking up his stone steps around the bend from his kitchen.

Waiting for my father to be gone, Chief Myles leans in towards me propping himself up with the back end of my chair whispering next to my ear, "Why were you snooping around at night?"

Taking in a deep breath, I reply hesitantly, "There is no law saying I can't."

Tugging the fleshy part of my ear, he snaps, "I don't care what is and is not illegal. It is foolish to be out at those hours. You hear? Many thieves and many unkindly sorts of people walk the streets at those hours."

Slapping his hand, I pull myself away from him by sliding over in my chair.

Slamming my face into the table, he growls, "Don't slap me when I'm speaking with you, boy."

Blood streams from my one nostril. I cup my hands over my face swelling with agonizing pain. Grappling me around the neck with his rough hand, Chief Myles leans closer to my ear whispering harshly, "Don't you ever go out at night. You hear?"

Coming back downstairs, my father is dressed in his plainer clothing made of basic brown cloth. Slapping me on the back, Chief Myles puts on a big smile saying, "Watch where you step, boy. You may break something more than your nose next time you trip. I hope our little talk though was a great benefit to you."

Still covering my nose, I glare at him with beady eyes nodding with reproach.

"Good. Well, General Damon I must be going now. My business here is complete."

"Thank you for dropping by, Chief Myles." Bowing respectfully, Chief Myles leaves with a salute.

Looking at me with slotted eyes, my father asks, "How did you fall?"

Debating inside myself whether or not to say the truth, I reply, "I stood up too quickly when Chief Myles asked me to, and I caught hold of the chair and fell." Whether I told the truth or not my father would never believe me.

"Hopefully that knocked some sense into you. Now, I want you to go to your room. You will not be out the rest of today. I need you here to know that you aren't out causing mischief. You hear?"

"Yes, sir." Slouching over, I walk to my room at the far corner of my father's home. Tenderly pressing shut my one nostril, I lie on my bed trying to drain the blood out of my nose onto the wooden floorboards.

Chief Myles deserves to die. I hope the Keeper's wife kills him. I hope she does.

Chapter 6

Waking up early, I sneak out of my father's house, still dressed in what I wore the day before. The sun, still a brilliant color of morning orange, warms the earth and opens the closed flowers in the dewy gardens around my father's place. Scurrying down the hallways of The Manor, I burst out the two giant doors that guard it from common peasants. Royal guards march across the top of The Manor, but none of them care to pay any attention to a sprinting child, especially a son of the highest ranked general. Arriving at Doctor Commons' office, I come to a halt heaving in deep breaths.

"Tommy, why are you running the streets like a madman?" Doctor Commons asks; he is attending to his roses out by his doorstep. They are pitiful looking things, pale around the edges and droopy like the ears on stray dogs, but Doctor Commons still waters them.

"I came running from The Manor. I hate trying to be all blasted respectful around all those breeds bates," I say, still breathing heavily.

"Now those breeds bates are our lords and generals who help lead this kingdom. They deserve our—"

"Enough already. I get it."

Scowling at me while holding his watering can, Doctor Commons chastises me, saying, "I was not finished. You do not interrupt your elders. Now as I was saying, they are our leaders and deserve our respect because of that. I know they can be rather..." pausing, Doctor Commons taps his chin then says, "rather unpleasant towards their people, but I'm sure things will change. Nonetheless they deserve respect."

"Oh, of course they do, Doc," I say sarcastically while rolling my eyes. Shaking his head, Doctor Commons empties his watering can and goes back inside his home. Following him, I sit down on his gnarly wooden stool and kick my feet against the wooden pegs. After putting away his watering can, Doctor Commons sits down beside me on his own personal stool.

"I heard they are announcing the new keeper today," he says. Pulling off his glasses, he wipes them down with the sleeve of his black cloak.

"Do you know who?" I ask.

Shaking his head, he replies, "There were no clues of who it may be, but I suppose whoever it is will be just as wise as the last."

"Just as wise? That fellow wound up in The Pit being buried by two drunks. He sounds like a fool to me."

"Watch yourself. Do not talk ill of the dead. Besides, that does not make one a fool. The fool is the one who hears wisdom, but rather than heeding to it runs from it knowing all so well he or she is making wrong choices."

Sighing, I reply, "I was jesting you," pausing, I think for a little then say, "maybe not completely. No one in their right mind hangs themselves. Only blasted cowards and whip-cats do that."

"You know so little. A tormented soul listens only to the demons inside that such actions seem rather welcoming."

"What demons would he have had?" I ask.

Shrugging, Doctor Commons replies, "I did not know him that well, but he always seemed like a rational fellow."

"It just doesn't make any sense."

Rising to his feet, Doctor Commons stretches before heading for the kitchen.

"Do you want any porridge?" he asks.

"I guess. What about our discussion?"

"What about it? There's not much left to be said. What is done is done."

Walking into Doctor Commons' kitchen, I watch him stir his porridge over the fire pit in a big black kettle. I told him many times before to buy a wood stove, but he never did. He likes traditional cooking, or so he says. I think it's because he doesn't want to bother with installing one. Sitting around his simple oak table that is well-polished with some sort of oily substance that makes it slick like ice, we eat our porridge.

"When is the new keeper being announced?" I ask, taking my last bite of gritty porridge.

Removing his glasses from his face, Doctor Commons sets them on the table by his bowl replying, "I believe twelve." Chuckling, he says, "I believe they picked that time purposely to make sure Jonah doesn't start another uproar."

"Probably," I say, putting my dishes in a basin filled with many other wooden and tin utensils.

Helping Doctor Commons around the office, I give medicine to those who request it and sweep up the floor with his broom every so often. Tedious work, but it gives me something to do other than roaming the streets aimlessly. Doctor Commons says those are the type of children that grow up to be thieves. I don't know if that's true, but I'll take his word for it. He's normally right.

Checking his pocket watch, Doctor Commons says, "Time to find out who was elected as our new keeper."

"I reckon some other farmer," I say, shrugging my shoulders.

"Do not degrade the worth of farmers; they are the staple of any city or kingdom. Besides, women on farms oftentimes are able to care for themselves if need be unlike most the women in this blasted city who without their man would not even know how to make ends meet."

"They also look like toothless boars."

Grabbing me by the shoulder, Doctor Commons whispers sharply, "Watch what you say. Your mother was a daughter of a farmer."

Glaring at him, I slap his arm snapping back, "I didn't mean her."

Clearing his throat, Doctor Commons steps back, pulls at the neck of his shirt, and replies, "I know. I am sorry for bringing her up. However, as a whole, farm women often times also have wider hips which is especially great for childbearing."

Closing my eyes, I shake my head saying, "Doc, just stop. I don't care about the blasted fish and bees or whatever the saying is. I'd much rather not bother with kids."

"Not as of yet," he comments with a smirk.

With a devilish grin, I reply, "Though I have a great yearning to find myself in bed with some mistress. I even have dreams."

It was Doctor Commons' turn to close his eyes and shake his head.

"Tommy, this is no joke. Do not create a game out of something so intimate. It's like laughing while the congregation is singing at church; it's very dishonoring."

"Yes, Doc. Just remember you started this blasted conversation."

"And I will end it. We must be going if we want to see the full Keeper Ceremony."

Leaving the office hastily, Doctor Commons and I walk swiftly towards city-square. The crowd there is mammoth, leaving barely any room for us to stand comfortably. As we arrive, Rey Oscar The Great, otherwise known as King Oscar, stands on top of The Square wearing his royal robes made of fine linen. Adjusting his golden crown with a navy-blue ruby in the center, he announces, "Welcome everyone to yet another Keeper Ceremony. Catastrophe has found its way into our tranquil kingdom, but from catastrophe we rise stronger. We pay our respects to the previous keeper who sadly breathed his last at the hand of himself. For what cause? No one knows, but whatever the cause was, it gave way to another man to find his purpose. Destiny and fate coincide as one. The fate of one awakes the destiny of another, as destiny also leads to fate. Before you, I stand proud to announce our next keeper of the farmers. He is a man of great strength, deed, and honor. I am proud to call upon Frederick Myles to be our next keeper of the farmers."

Clapping reluctantly, the audience greets Frederick as any would greet a stranger — with suspicion. Many people whisper among themselves, some roll their eyes, and others laugh. Their applause is a mask for their true thoughts.

Shaking the hand of King Oscar, Frederick, a tall handsome man with long blond hair and dreamy blue eyes looks nothing like an average farmer. He is much too fair. Raising his hand in the air, Frederick silences the crowd. Then he begins his speech by saying, "I am honored to be here. I am not keen to speaking before so many people, especially those I do not know well. However, if my few years of schooling taught me anything it is to face your fears so that you may become stronger. That is why I'm here today. I would like to face my fears. I am not much of a leader, but I am a man of just judgement and wise counsel. I will keep up the law and not disown those who are weak. I speak for my fellow farmers not because I could use the extra gold, but rather because they are the voice unheard. If my own brother would be found out of line, beating one of my own I would have him thrown into a cell. If he would be found murdering one of my people, I would have him strung up like any other murder. An eye for an eye and a tooth for a tooth, as the saying goes. Justice does not miss any, and chastisement favors none. I will speak for my people on their behalf so that they may not be disowned and that they may not be herded like cattle into a certain niche to fit the criteria a certain tyrant laid out for them. I will carry this gauntlet with honor and with humility as I represent those on the other side of the wall." Stepping down from The Square, Frederick could be seen wiping a tear from his eye.

"Frederick, the ceremony is not yet over. Please, come back onto The Square so that you may be properly given the role of keeper of the farmers," says King Oscar urgently with red cheeks. He keeps his back straight so to draw as little attention as possible to himself. He does not want to be made a fool by a farmer's error.

"Forgive me, Your Majesty," says Frederick to humor King Oscar as he jumps back onto The Square. He must know the king cares little about him. I'm sure his extravagant speech, different from most speeches delivered by former keepers, was him simply trying to gain more power by proving how well-mannered he is. To seem less like a farmer and more like a representative. Standing next to King Oscar, Frederick does have a sort of natural royal look to him.

Clearing his throat and pulling at his robes, King Oscar speaks up, "It is quite all right. Now if you will, please bow."

Kneeling, Frederick bows his head.

Given a golden ear ring from one of his advisors, King Oscar pierces Frederick's ear, announcing, "Behold the keeper of the farmers."

Applauding again, the crowd cheers with approval. His speech must have swayed the audience. It gave them hope. False hope, but hope nonetheless. Rising to his feet, Frederick steps down from The Square and cuts through the crowd, not even acknowledging their presence.

Chapter 7

"Believe me when I say that The Beast's spirit is alive and well," Jonah says from The Square. A small group stands before him, but most ignore him as they grab what they need from the markets. They have given up on taunting him. "Yesterday the new keeper delivered his speech about justice, but how can there be justice when everyone ignores the true sower of evil?"

"The keeper is just a blasted title for an overpaid beer maker. He ain't nobody important to listen to," says one of the few men who stand before Jonah. Most of the people standing before him are dirty beggars, stupors, or prostitutes. It's the most entertainment they have that is legal.

"That is exactly why you should listen! Those who are lowly quickly rise up when faced with tribulation and given ambition. The Beast's spirit provides both. He creates the tribulation and stirs up ambition so that those that are his victims may die at each other's hands."

"You speak of parables. Talk less of fables and more of my talk so that I may think of what you talk," babbles one drunk, shuffling his feet like an overweight ass. His eyes are cloudy. Looking at Jonah, he seems to lose focus of him every time he sways. His eyes get big then they shrink. His eyes get big again then they shrink again. So forth and so on.

"Yeah, you're too much smart. Ain't I going to understand you. Unless The Beast was right in bed with me, and he better pay his gold if so," squawks a skimpily

43

dressed harlot with her brown wavy hair hanging down to her buttocks.

"Just because you don't see him does not mean he is not here. Those you lie in bed with probably are well acquainted with him, though he be far from their knowledge," replies Jonah, looking directly at the harlot.

Jabbing a finger at Jonah, she snaps back, "You stay out of my business. Ain't easy to learn nothing. Easy to get a man, though, when the body's fine. Lend me ten pieces of gold and I'll show you what I mean."

Loosening the top of her dress, she lets Jonah see her breasts, but he quickly spins around saying, "I will not partake in the works of the Devil, nor will I defile myself and be susceptible to The Beast."

Most of the men around her begin to reach out towards her with longing eyes, but she quickly hisses, "Not 'less you pay." Tightening the strings at her breasts, she hastily covers herself up. Then turning back to Jonah says, "Ain't you know the way life works?"

Still with his back facing the prostitute, he replies, "Yes, and for a marriage bed much of life should be shared, but fornication at the expense of hell is a much too high a price."

"Now you look here, you bas—"

"Doctor! We need Doctor Commons! Clear out of the way!" cry two guards bounding into city-square with their carriage practically on two wheels. Screeching into Doctor Commons' lane, they disappear.

What could that be for? I ask myself. Normally people don't gallop to Doctor Commons unless it's an emergency. Seeing that they had a wagon must mean someone was in the back lying down

Running for Doctor Commons, I arrive there to see the carriage empty. The horses aren't even tied up. The guards must have been in a hurry. Rushing inside, I stop at the opening of the door. On Doctor Commons' patient bed is Chief Myles with what looks like an arrow going through his left shoulder. Blood oozes from the wound and he fades out of consciousness with his bloody tongue hanging out of his mouth. Yanking out the arrow, Doctor Commons reaches for a tall bottle filled with a cloudy fluid. Pouring it onto the wound, Doctor Common quickly plugs the glass. Chief Myles groans as the medicine bubbles. Splashing a little bit of mercury onto a cloth, Doctor Commons tenderly applies it to the wound. I see the focus in Doctor Commons' eyes. His fingers are still, but his tapping foot reflects his urgency. However, it is too late; Chief Myles' eyes glaze over and his body goes limp. The guards standing by his side are cursing underneath their breaths as they hold their thighs tightly. Chief Myles lets out a light sigh as he slips into oblivion. Resting his forehead on Chief Myles' sternum, Doctor Commons mumbles to himself before getting up to put away his tools.

"Damn the bastard who shot that arrow!" the guard closest to me growls, marching out the door. The other one stands still just staring at Chief Myles. It's Jonathan. It's a cocktail stare. A stare filled with rage and spiked with shock.

"It was a tramp for sure. The keeper's wife swore she was going to kill him. Now look. He is dead. That homely wheat shucking bastard," Jonathan snarls, "She's going to be squared up." Marching out the door, he hops onto the carriage along with his friend and rides off towards The Manor.

Turning towards Doctor Commons, I ask, "What do you think those weasels are gonna do?"

Throwing his dirty rags into an empty basin, he hesitates before replying, "They are going to have that lady hanged."

"They have no proof it was her."

"They don't need any. All they need is cause."

"That's not right!" I shout, punching my hand.

Slamming down his glasses on his work table, Doctor Commons snaps back, "Neither is an arrow to the chest! Neither is any of this bloody circus we play in!

Nothing is fair. Nothing." Trumping upstairs, Doctor Commons doesn't turn around once. His focus has shifted from Myles to disappointment. A rotten disappointment turned inward. I let him go upstairs without a reply. I have nothing left to say to him.

Staring at Chief Myles' body, I find words I want to share with him. They aren't kind, but they feel justified. I whisper, "You got what was fair though, you weasel."

* * *

Before dusk fall, the town gathers together in two large columns leaving an opening in the middle as wide as the road that leads to the main gate. Already on top of the square is the executioner with a jester's mask over his face and a black hood over his head. That is to make sure no one who is friends with the person being hanged has any intentions to murder the executioner. A trumpet sounds. Following the trumpet boy dressed in all black are two guards mounted on horses pulling an iron cage on wheels behind them. Inside is the former keeper's wife chained up so that she is forced into a kneeling position with her head high and hands behind her back.

Screaming, she rams the side of the cage with her shoulder, "I didn't kill that blasted fellow! I didn't kill him! This is injustice! This is damn tyranny!"

Silence plagues the crowd as everyone watches with empty stares. Even some of the guards spread across the front of the columns look sheepishly at her with slouched shoulders like they pity her or feel guilty. Maybe both. Biting at her chains, she futilely tries to get loose.

Reaching the front of The Square, the guards come to a stop, but the woman in the cage doesn't. She continues to slam herself against the solid barred walls. I grit my teeth. Her arm looks swollen and blood leaks from her mouth. Seething, she doesn't think, just acts. She wants to be free, but she won't be. I sigh. I hate this. I hate having to watch this.

Rising onto The Square, King Oscar, wearing his gray robes of mourning, announces, "Today we execute Evelynn Jade for the murder of Chief Myles."

"I didn't kill him you wretched powder boy! I didn't kill him!" Evelynn shrieks, snarling like a rabid dog.

Fixing his black crown with only one diamond-shaped ruby in the center of it, worn only for executions, King Oscar continues on, "She has done wrong in the sight of the crown and the public and will receive what she is rightly owed. An eye for an eye." Stepping down from The Square, he doesn't leave the dagger throwing glare of Evelynn. She goes silent as the guards take her out of her cage and drag her up The Square steps. Never once does she stop scowling at King Oscar. Her eyes are beady, concentrated on him like a long, thin spear. Setting her on her knees, the guards walk away, allowing the executioner to do his work.

"Hurry there now," King Oscar says, scratching at his throat. Evelynn doesn't say a word, but just stares menacingly at him. It doesn't even look like she's breathing. Her hatred is her breath. Wrapping the noose around Evelynn's neck, the executioner tightens the knot so that Evelynn strains to breathe. Stepping down from The Square, the executioner finds the board sticking out from the platform of The Square and, pulling it all the way out, releases the swinging trap door beneath Evelynn. Falling, Evelynn gags as the rope pulls up on her neck, strangling her. She swings side to side gagging, but never once stops glaring at King Oscar. She swings herself so that she can keep her eyes on him. Fidgeting with his crown, King Oscar tries to look away, but her eyes are like a harpoon; they draw him in. Her eyes are steady, ominously steady, until her body goes limp and her eyes flutter shut.

The trumpet sounds. The execution is over.

Chapter 8

At church early in the morning, I nearly fall asleep. The priest speaks slowly and in a monotone voice that has little life. Not a single soul there feels alive. An execution yesterday and a long, drawn out sermon today breeds jadedness. Sleeping, men in the pews snore until their wives nudge them, but those wives, too, would pay to be anywhere else. Looking around, I don't see anyone who seems gladly attentive except Jonah who sits in the very front pew. I sit two pews behind him. Leaning in with his elbows on his knees, Jonah stares at the priest as if he were a beautiful dame when he is, on the contrary, an old wrinkly man with a giant golden cross necklace hanging down to his waist.

Inspecting the stained-glass windows, I pass the time by counting all the crosses inside the giant sanctuary until the service is closed with prayer. Everyone leaves as quick as they can.

Walking behind me, Doctor Commons checks his pocket watch, saying, "Started at seven and ended at quarter before eleven. That was awfully long."

Nodding in agreement, I reply, "I nearly walked out on my own."

"You wouldn't have dared. Your father sits right by the sanctuary door anyhow."

"That is true."

At the sanctuary door stands the priest with his hands out to shake the hands of those who pass.

"Thank you for speaking today, Father John," Doctor Commons says, mustering up a smile.

"You're welcome, my son. I pray that you have a blessed day as you walk in the way of our Lord and Savior," Father John replies with a raspy, antiquated voice.

I simply wave as I hurry down the steps onto the cobblestone street below. The church is on the west side of the city, farthest from The Manor.

"Thomas!" my father calls. He stands before me about twenty paces away. Trudging over there, I look up at him timidly.

"Yes?" I reply.

"Yes what?"

Sighing, I reply, "Yes, sir?"

"Better. I will be busy the next few days as I attend to a—" pausing, my father looks at the sky and then back at me saying, "a few propositions King Oscar has for me."

"OK."

"I better not hear that you have fallen into mischief again. Keep your nose clean. Good day." Marching towards his horse, my father rides off for The Manor.

Resting his hand on my shoulder, Doctor Commons says, "You can stay with me, Tommy."

I nod absently. My father disappears behind a distant stone building with me watching him. I don't watch sad, angry, or even frustrated. I watch empty. This is the life I was given. I might as well live with Doctor Commons and become his son. My own father doesn't take care of me. I would have most likely been dead by now if it wasn't for Doctor Commons.

Walking into city-square, I look up at the gallows. Still hanging there bluer than azurite is Evelynn. It is a crime to bury someone on Sunday because it is meant to be a holy day. However, it is against tradition to bury someone on the day of their execution. Therefore, Evelynn still hangs there with her swollen tongue hanging from the side of her mouth as flocks of crows pick and scratch at her pale flesh, constantly squabbling with each other over scraps.

"Beastly creatures," Doctor Commons mutters, "They have no control. They flock upon the weak and devour them till there is nothing left."

Nodding, I slide my feet across the cobblestone, slouched over.

"It looks like Olson is at my door again," Doctor Commons mumbles. Looking up, I notice a scruffy man sleeping up against Doctor Commons' door. He is thin with long, lanky arms and wears nothing but his undergarments. His eyelids are dark like a starless night, and they hang low like anchors.

Kicking him, Doctor Commons rouses Olson who snorts loudly and slams his hands against the wooden door.

"What!? Who is it!?" he shouts. Looking up at us, he wipes his sweaty brow with relief. "Commons, you scared me out of my wits."

"What wits?" Doctor Commons remarks with a huff.

"Don't be like that now. You know I was with you at the same university."

"Yes, and then you became a lousy bum as soon as you sold your trading posts."

Shaking a bony finger at Doctor Commons, Olson says, "Look, Commons. I ain't poor, just look it. I ain't one to waste my earnings."

"Is that why I smell alcohol all over you?"

"I drink because there is nothing else to do besides at night when the strumpets are out for the grabbing," Olson says, winking at me. His smile is ugly. He's got a face only a mother can love.

"You are a wretched fool."

"No, I'm a hedonist and troubled fool."

Sighing, Doctor Commons rolls his crystal blue eyes, replying, "What trouble do you have now?"

Dramatically grabbing his chest and throwing his other hand up against his forehead, Olson moans, "My head, my heart, my body. I am just always so sore these days. With migraines like a—"

"Drunk," Doctor Commons remarks with a snarky grin.

Removing his crummy hand from his crinkled forehead, Olson replies with a nasty look, "I was going to say horseman without a saddle," flailing his hands up at his face again like an exasperated mother does when her kids break her favorite vase, he continues, "so if you could find it in your heart to spare me some of that fine medicine you have at hand. I will be on my way."

"You are a thin-skinned suckling," Doctor Commons mutters, swinging his door open so it hits Olson. Stumbling backwards, Olson grabs the side of his face as he whines like a lost child when hardly a scratch is on his cheek.

"You're a terrible doctor," he says, still gingerly dabbing where the door hit him.

"Now you may actually need the tonic you so desire." Strutting inside, Doctor Commons takes off his suit coat, throwing it onto his nearby coat rack. Stumbling inside, Olson steadies himself with the gnarly stool I normally sit on.

"I ought to get a double portion," he says, scratching his forehead.

"Not unless you brought enough silver for it."

Reaching both hands into his loincloth, Olson twists his fingers around like a pretzel to untie his money bag which he keeps up against his thigh.

Pulling out the tarnished leather pouch, he grins, "That way no one dares to snitch off me."

Scrunching up his nose, Doctor Commons puts his glasses on, outstretching his hand, "The coins only. That will be twenty pieces if you want a double portion."

Fingering through his coins, Olson hands Doctor Commons twenty pieces of silver. Counting it out, Dr. Commons nods his head, reaching into his medicine cabinet and grabbing two thimble-size glass bottles colored a deep ocean blue.

"He pays for those small things?" I ask, squinting my eyes.

"It balances his humors," Doctor Commons replies, "His phlegm is out of proportion, according to him. I would say his brain is out of proportion."

"You know I'm mentally fine. I was smarter than you. Remember? I use to always outwit you at Cambridge."

Ignoring his remarks, Doctor Commons hands him the two bottles.

Taking them anxiously, Olson says, "Yes. A mixture of grounded wormwood along with minty water. Such delight is rarely found, especially in these troubled days."

"Troubled days?" I ask.

"Yes. The Beast will be upon us before we know it."

"You're a fool, Olson," Doctor Commons grunts, placing the silver he received into his personal money bag made from fine silk.

"Not a fool. I merely listen and observe. I have been hearing *voices*," he says, saying "voices" like he's some sort of ghoul. He grins that ugly grin with his two crooked front teeth sticking out. The odd black bags underneath his eyes look a shade darker. Getting thicker, the air sticks to my throat.

"In your head," Doctor Commons remarks.

"In my chest. I can feel it," leaning in towards me like a vampire leaning in for the kill, Olson closes one eye whispering, "Beware The Beast."

Shuddering, I remain silent. Hackling, Olson backs away, shaking his glass bottles.

"Enough of that. Now get out of here, you goat," Doctor Commons says, jabbing his glasses at Olson.

"As you wish," he replies, bowing so low he nearly touches the floor. Looking at me again he smiles connivingly, "Beware The Beast." Shutting the door behind him, he still cackles loudly.

"Fool," mutters Doctor Commons, walking back into his kitchen.

Wiping my nose, I can still smell the musty alcohol from Olson's lips. *Beware? What even is The Beast? What even is it? Or should I just beware? Beware.* I think this to myself, but don't say. Doctor Commons would think me a fool for even wondering what Olson meant, but I do wonder. *Beware.*

Chapter 9

Someone must have taken down Evelynn's body early in the morning. When Jonah's midday rant began, her body was nowhere to be seen. Someone couldn't stand to see her rotting corpse another day. Neither could I.

"How many more must die before you heed to what I say?" Jonah asks nearly in tears. His flabby chin jiggles up and down as he tries his best to refrain from crying.

Throwing a bloody rag onto Jonah's leather sandals, the butcher with a cleaver in hand grumbles like he has rocks in his throat, "Use this you weak-legged hedge-born."

Bending over to pick up the filthy rag, Jonah sniffles, throwing the rag onto the street. Those near it clear out of the way like it is a virulent poison.

"You make a mockery out of me," Jonah whimpers, tightening his belt made of twine around his gray tunic.

Picking up the rag with his meaty hands, the butcher stabs his cleaver at Jonah with the stare of an enraged turkey buzzard.

"Better watch it, doughboy, or I'll make more than a mockery out of you."

"What have I done to offend you?"

"I salt my meat twice a day now 'cuz of your foolery. My people waste their time on your blasted prophecies that turn out to be nothing except nonsense."

"I must speak what's on my mind."

"I must get gold. Either way, we both need something." Cutting the air with his cleaver, the butcher sticks it into The Square splitting the end of one wooden plank.

Jumping backwards, Jonah trips over his tunic, crashing onto his back like a lame horse. Laughing loudly, the crowd jeers at him calling him names and tossing food at him. Rolling onto his feet, Jonah balls up his fists cracking his knuckles.

"Tonight, your idiocrasy will be punished by heavenly fire. Like lightning from the sky, it will rain down!" he shouts, knocking his fist together like he's beating a drum.

Yanking his cleaver out from The Square, the butcher spits on Jonah's feet, shoving those around him out of his way using his massive body to his advantage.

He is a hunk of meat. I think to myself.

"The Beast is not going to be kind any longer. The tenth day is arriving," Jonah growls menacingly, silencing the crowd. Marching off The Square, Jonah leaves in silence being jeered by none.

"Oh, joy. I wonder what will happen tomorrow," Doctor Commons mumbles beside me. "If another person dies, I will contemplate moving to another city."

Looking up at him, I notice the corner of Doctor Commons' thin lips dropping so that they seem to be running down his face. His visage looks like a rippling brook with small waves of wrinkles crashing over each other.

"Where would you move to, though?" I ask, trying my best not to appear sad about the thought of him leaving. I would move with him. He's all I really got.

Smiling warmly, he says, "Do not fear, Tommy. I do not plan to leave. However, there is another city a two-day journey away which I could trek towards."

"What's it called?"

"Liberty."

Rolling my eyes, I sigh, "Really?"

"I am serious. It is called Liberty."

"Why, I never heard of it."

"Because King Oscar has bad relations with King Kristo of Liberty. The only reason we are not in the middle of a war is because Liberty is far larger than our small kingdom. Kristo has five times more soldiers than we have."

Scratching my scruffy head, I ask, "Why don't they raid us?"

"They are not monsters. Kristo is not about inflicting his will over others. Only if he is provoked will he conquer. However, I could see a day when all fall beneath his reign."

"Why is that?"

Looking down at his pocket watch, Dr. Commons lets out a choppy sigh that's almost like a sob, "Time is a peculiar fiend. Soon it will be Kristo's time to claim what belongs to him and set it right."

Frowning, I reply, "What?"

Shaking his head, Doctor Commons smiles, fighting back watery tears lingering in the corners of his pink eyes. They're genuine tears. The ones that glisten with heartache not strained by simple infirmities.

"I'm sorry. Don't mind me," Doctor Commons croaks, clearing his throat he continues, "I mean let us head back to my office. Certain patients may be arriving soon."

"But—"

"No buts, Tommy. Let us leave."

Looking back at city-square one last time, I watch a couple young boys, no older than eight, chase after each other. The one is laughing hysterically as the other looks sad with red rimmed eyes. They run in circles, but I see that the teary-eyed boy will not catch the laughing one who is a head shorter. However, tripping over his own scaly feet, the laughing boy falls face first into the cobblestone, scraping his soft cheeks. Blood trickles down the fallen boy's scuffed cheek. Reaching the fallen boy, the teary eyed one tries to help his playmate up, but the one on the ground smacks him instead, balling loudly. The one who just earlier was laughing tried so hard to stay ahead of his friend, but because of his arrogance he fell.

"Tommy, come along now," Doctor Commons says glancing back towards me over his shoulder. He ignores the children.

Peeling my eyes away from the two boys, I follow Doctor Commons in a daze. The world spins in circles around me, but I do not notice. I am trapped in my own world. I am in another place. My mind absorbs me.

Chapter 10

Thunder roars after the first strike of the church bell. It is midnight, but no moon is out. The towering clouds above cloak the orange circle in the sky. Gazing out the window by my bed, I stare out into the stormy void. I never could sleep well, but especially not when it is storming. Not even Doctor Commons himself is asleep. I can hear him pacing downstairs. His feet scuffle across the wooden boards, but most of the noise he makes is drowned out by the thundering storm. Gripping onto the side of my bed, I count the number of times the clouds roar with rage. It's a terrifying phenomenon I never learned to enjoy properly. Storms always make me feel small and skittish, like my father does, so I have a certain distaste for them.

A flash of pure energy surges through the air and strikes an opposing cloud casting a bright white light over the city. Following the flash, a loud clap of thunder shakes the entire house. Staring wide-eyed up at the black monster in the sky, I shake nervously.

Silence falls.

A blinding streak of light strikes down into city-square. A blaze of fire erupts but then dissipates into a cloud of smoke. The whole earth trembles and cries out in pain as the tyrant above laughs with his deep gruff voice tearing apart every inch of me. Falling over, my head hits my pillow. Rolling a little farther, I nearly fall onto the floor, but I manage to catch myself at the last moment. Heavy footsteps come running up the stairs. Flinging open my door, Doctor Commons looks out the window with a face of pure terror. His mouth dangles and his skin appear to melt.

"Like lightning," he whispers, "impossible."

Pushing myself back onto my knees, I ask, "Still some fantasies?"

Looking at me with disbelief, he replies, "I don't know. It does not make sense. That is the butcher's shop."

Looking out the window, I squint my eyes. A little fire crackles on the roof of a now crisp butcher's shop. I can't see very well, but I can see many chunks of stones scattered all around. There must be a giant gap in the roof somewhere.

"Is he an actual prophet?" I ask, quivering.

Doctor Commons brushes his hair back while shaking his head. A hint of fear gleams in his eyes as another flash of lightning races through the sky into the dark vacuity above. Shaking his head to erase the thought that cross his head as well as mine, he replies, "Impossible. Impossible. He cannot be serious. He cannot."

"Then how did he see this?" I ask, pointing at the wreckage outside.

"He saw nothing, but simply blurted nonsense out of rage. He is a mad fellow with a hair issue. He cannot possibly be a prophet."

"Why? Because the University of Cambridge said so?"

Glaring at me, Doctor Commons snarls, "Do not let foolish pride and blind mockery intercept your judgement and respect."

"You're afraid because you don't understand."

"Silence yourself or you'll become exactly what that mad fellow has become. A lunatic."

A loud clap of thunder erupts across the heavens causing Doctor Commons to jump. Gazing out the window, he shakes his head while rubbing his saggy eyes.

"What?" I ask.

"This storm will wreak havoc," he says.

"Why?"

Staring at me with watery eyes, he replies, "Because he will get them to believe anything now."

* * *

"How did you know?" cries a grayed-hair woman with an infant in the crook of her arms.

"I saw what was to come. What is to come. No longer can any of you sit here and simply accept death," Jonah proclaims, waving his hands in the air.

"What are we to do?" shouts the dame with beautiful black hair.

"Yeah," the blacksmith bellows.

"What I have told you to do. Fight the ways of The Beast."

"What is this Beast?" asks a fellow dressed in tattered robes that look suitable for cows to sleep on.

"Have you people ignored me till this day? The Beast is every possible evil you can think of. Legions bow before him and darkness is spewed out of his mouth. He inhabits every mind and takes captive every child. No families are out of his grasp unless they cling onto wisdom. Unless they turn towards the heavens and pray. Unless they avoid the company of fools. They will perish. His end goal is death."

"Like the fellow in ashes?" asks the blacksmith. He points towards the butcher shop which now looks like a rock slide went through it. No one has searched for his body yet, but most everyone assumes he has died. Everyone keeps their distance from the building's remains as if it is a leper, afraid they may catch its disease.

"Yes. He gave up the ghost living in vanity, but none of you have to face the same fate."

Standing on the outskirts of the city-square, I watch the crowd steadily get larger till there is no room for anyone to walk through. Everyone seems to be interested in what Jonah has to say now. I suppose lightning from heaven would cause any to wonder if the words of a so-called prophet are true.

"Have you seen The Beast?" asks a woman who I cannot see.

Jonah replies, "In dreams and here. I see him everywhere."

"Lead us against him!" shouts a drunk who doesn't stand too far from me. Waving his bottle of liquor in the air, he tips it back towards his mouth but misses, spilling it all over his gray tunic.

"I am no warrior."

"You are a god!" shouts another random person.

"I pray you do not call me that I—"

"You see the unseen!" shouts another.

"You have been sent!" shouts another and another until the whole crowd is chanting together, "You have been sent! You have been sent!"

Shoving me out of the way, three guards with swords drawn march towards the crowd shouting, "Get out of the way! Make room so we can pass! Go home!"

The chanting crowd turns towards the guards shouting back at them, screaming various of curses, remarks, and phrases not meant for children's ears. Following the guards are the two drunks I saw bury the former keeper. Along with them are shovels and the same wagon they toted last time I saw them.

"Make way, boy. We made to clear stones for butcher," says the taller drunk, knocking me out of the way with his bony shoulder.

"Yeah, boy," says the other following behind him. They both reek with sweat and alcohol. Their hair jumps with lice and their faces are scruffier than most animals. Stopping behind the three guards ahead of me, they sit down on their wagon taking swigs from the same large bottle.

"Clear way now!" the guards shout, "We must search out the wreckage!"

"Go to hell!" someone cries from the crowd. Advancing towards the guards, the crowd gets louder, waving their fists in the air along with whatever they are holding such as clubs, knives, and assortments of fruits and vegetables. Swinging their swords in the air, the guards try to stand their ground, but a stone clobbers the middle guard in the head, knocking him over. Rushing the guards, the crowd swallows them whole. They tear and rip at their leather armor. I spot one of the guard's swords skid across the cobblestone street. Screams of bloody murder slice through the air. Wiggling his way out of the clawing crowd, a guard no bigger than me scrambles away, leaving the other two to die.

I stand still like a statue. I'm grounded in place. Grounded in horror.

A stampede of horses come galloping down the street behind me. Turning around, I spot my father on the horse in the very front. He wears his full iron armor looking like an elegant warrior riding off into battle. Looks can be deceiving.

The crowd spots the army of horses and men coming their way. Running in different directions, they all flee shouting curses. I'm still frozen. I just witnessed a real-life mob. Lying paralyzed at the edge of city-square, the two guards are covered in bruises. Blood paints their faces and shards of bone stick out from their bodies. There is no possible way they are still alive. However, the same two drunks still sit at their wagon like nothing happened. The shorter, less dominant of the two shakes the bottle in his hand trying to get the last drop with his tongue.

"You drunken fools, search that wreckage!" shouts my father from his black horse.

"Yes, sir," they both reply, pulling their wagon slowly. The shorter one is still trying to get that last drop until the taller one slaps it out of his hand, shattering glass everywhere.

"You two," my father says, pointing at two soldiers on his left also wearing iron armor, "take care of those fallen guards."

"Yes, sir," they reply, trotting over towards the two corpses.

Shooting daggers at me with his eyes, my father trots my way, growling, "What are you doing with these bloody rats? They kill two guards and you stand there foolishly. How will you make a royal guard as a spineless coward?"

"How am I supposed to stop a riot by myself?" I protest, jabbing my chest with my pointer finger. I can feel my ribs tremble reminding me of how weak I am.

"Get yourself killed if you have to. Nothing is worse than a coward."

"What about a callous ass?" I snap back. As the words leave my mouth, I regret everything I just said. Lowering himself down from his horse, my father pulls out his sword from its sheath. Marching up to me with a straight face about to burst open with raging fumes, he doesn't stop glaring at me. Quivering, I try my best not to run. Grabbing hold of the back of his sword, he swings clobbering my jaw with the iron hilt. Before I can even scream, he comes back around hitting me again on the other side of my jaw so that if feels like it's going to fall off. Covering my mouth, I try to contain the blood gushing out from between my teeth and the tears on the verge of running down my cheeks.

Leaning in towards my face, my father snarls, "I was not the one who killed your mother, now was I? It was you! You killed her at birth! Do not ever call me an ass again!"

Nodding, I give up on containing the blood, letting it stream down my chin onto my dirty tunic.

"Now clean yourself up, you dirty rat," he says, shoving me out of his way.

Stumbling, I catch myself on a nearby wall. My jaw hangs on a thread as every part of my face swells with agonizing pain. Struggling to get to Doctor Commons' house, I fall at his door weakly, hitting it with my fist. Opening the door, Doctor Commons looks down at me with a gasp and quickly carries me inside. The pain absorbs me, my vision weakens, and time seems to slow down as I fade out of consciousness in Doctor Commons' arms.

Chapter 11

Awakening, I try to move my jaw, but I can't. It feels like it's tied shut. Moving my hand, I can feel my bed beneath me. Pushing myself up against the wall, I see nothing but darkness. Patting my jaw, I feel a thin piece of cloth that wraps around the bottom of my chin up towards the top of my head. Groaning, I feel aching pain consume my face. My door opens and Doctor Commons walks in with a small bowl of steaming broth.

"Finally awake, I see," he says with a smile. Setting down the bowl on the nightstand beside my bed, he bends over and unties the cloth around my head. "Don't move your jaw too much now."

As he pulls the cloth away from my face, I slowly move my jaw side to side. A few times I hear it crunch, but eventually it moves smoothly, as smooth as a bruised jaw can move; however, there are still many pangs of pain that hit my body every time I move it. A constant throb where my father struck me reminds me of his cruelty.

"Your jaw was not broken, thankfully. However, it did swell up."

Rubbing my cheek absentmindedly, I feel my fingers climb over my face like it is a mountain.

"That bloody fellow is wreaking havoc. I hope he gets run in," Doctor Commons mutters, pulling a bottle of ointment out of his coat pocket.

"The people aren't innocent," I whisper, wincing with every word I say.

Sighing, Doctor Commons nods his head saying, "That is true. Our kingdom was bound to break apart at some point."

"What do you mean?"

"Moral depravity, power struggles, and an uneven distribution of wealth creates space for revolution to develop. Jonah is just a catalyst."

Sipping on broth, I try to figure what Jonah will influence the people to do, but my head hurts too much to think.

The clock strikes twelve. Outside the stars glimmer over the city.

"How long have I been sleeping?" I ask.

"I gave you a dose of opium. After that, you slept for hours," he says, gently rubbing his white ointment that reminds me of hot wax on my cheeks. It burns, then cools, then hardens over my face like a glaze made for a cake.

"What is that?" I ask.

"It's a simple ointment made to relieve skin irritation and any pain caused by swelling."

"Oh, that's good."

Closing my eyes, I focus my attention on the gentle touch of Doctor Commons and how the ointment, now cool and hard, makes my wound feel less painful. Breaking my tranquil rest, loud shouting outside resounds throughout the city. Pulling back from me, Doctor Commons puts on his bottle-size glasses so he can see out the window by my bed. Fighting a terrible headache, I sit up to look outside as well. A group of three men with torches beat a woman dressed in a transparent silky undergarment only harlots wear. They are only a few steps from Doctor Commons' office. The men are disguised behind large black cloaks. Two of the men hold torches as the other one socks the woman in her face.

"You blasted wanton, how dare you defy the sent one!?" the beater shouts.

68

In between sobs, the woman cries, "I ain't the only one who didn't believe."

"You're going to be devoured by hell's dogs, whore!" Throwing the woman up against the neighboring house, the beater rips at the woman's long wavy hair. His bulky arms glisten with sweat in the light of the torches as the sleeves of his cloak slide down towards his shoulders. "I'll lead you to damnation, bitch." Opening the door to the house, the beater along with his partners trump inside with the woman, closing the door behind them.

"What do we do?" I ask, looking at Doctor Commons with wide eyes.

Shaking his head, he takes off his glasses rubbing the bridge of his nose, "Go to sleep."

"Didn't you hear them?"

"What are we to do? The Gate House is a long way from here, and chances are one of those men is a weasel. They are well known for sleeping with harlots. It serves as a payment to keep them from chirping on the prostitutes on the streets."

"It isn't right."

"Such is life."

Closing the door to my room, Doctor Commons walks away. I listen to his footsteps proceed down the steps, still in shock he could let something so awful happen. Glancing out the window, I glimpse at the stars above, praying that when I wake up nothing too bad happens.

Looking down at the house the woman was dragged into, I think to myself, *just forget it*. But how can one simply forget that?

* * *

"Tommy," Doctor Commons whispers, nudging my shoulder.

Waking up, I reply, "Yes."

"Come downstairs right now," he says. There's tension in his voice. Just a slip away from calm to berserk. His eyes are very alert and glued on me. I recognize this is not a time to make a joke. Getting out of bed, I quickly follow Doctor Commons downstairs, not bothering to change out of my nightgown. At the bottom of the steps are three guards dressed in their typical beige uniforms.

"What did you see, boy?" the guard in the middle asks with a deep, trembling voice. His shoulders are broad and his figure is well-filled. At his disposal he has a sword which hangs by his side in his sheath, but the others carry no weapons.

"Last night?" I ask timidly, my voice cracking.

"Precisely."

"I think I know what you mean. Well three fellows, I mean men, were beating a woman—"

"All three?"

"Well, only one. The others held torches."

"Go on," the middle guard replies, grabbing a piece of thick paper from his partner to the right and a quill from his partner on the left. The guard on the left has in hand a small inkwell for the middle guard to dip his quill in. They seem more like servants than guards.

"Well, they dragged her into our neighbor's house."

Looking over at Doctor Commons, the middle guard asks, "He lives with you?"

Doctor Commons replies quickly, saying, "Only when his father is not available."

"Who is his father?"

"The High General Damon."

Looking at me with wonder, the middle guard for the first time gives a hint at a smile raising the corners of his mouth.

"I thought you look familiar despite your chipmunk cheeks," he says, chuckling. His snickering seems to shake the whole room.

"Yes, sir," I say, not knowing what else to reply with. I feel like I should feel embarrassed or angry by him calling me chipmunk cheeks, but I'm too nervous to feel anything else. So nervous I feel even a little queasy.

Sobering up, the middle guard asks, "Anything else that you saw?"

"No, sir," I reply, "but what happened that you are here?" I already know what happened. I just have to hear it myself.

"That woman was murdered, but beforehand it would seem she was forced to sleep with the men or man. She was a well-known harlot. She was acclaimed to have jewels for breasts by those who done business with her."

"How would you know?" Doctor Commons asks curtly.

"Other witnesses," the middle guard snarls, glaring at Doctor Commons with snake eyes.

"Would make sense," Doctor Commons replies with biting sarcasm as he rubs his glasses with a white handkerchief.

"Watch yourself, Doc," the middle guard growls, tapping the hilt of his sword with his right hand.

Eyeing up the guard's sword, Doctor Commons huffs, lowering his glasses onto his patients' bed.

"We shall leave you two alone now," the middle guard says to me, ignoring Doctor Commons.

As soon as they close the door, Doctor Commons shakes his head, saying, "Those blasted weasels are the most two-faced people. I cannot stand them."

"Definitely rude," I whisper, rubbing my cheeks. They ache tremendously. I am convinced I will never know how it is to be comfortable again. Constant aching will become my comfort.

"Rude is an understatement."

Picking up his glasses, Doctor Commons walks towards the medicine cabinet. The door rattles.

"Who could that be?" Doctor Commons grumbles, setting down his glasses next to a weird, gray, ointment.

Before he even reaches the door, whoever it is bursts inside. It's Jonathan. His leather armor drips with blood. Leaking from a gash in his head is a crimson trail leading down to the corner of his mouth. His eyes battle to stay straight. They jump back into his skull, then they go straight again. Trembling, his fingers race back and forth.

Falling at Doctor Commons' feet, he shouts, "Damn those plebeians! Those low lives!" His voice is hoarse like he's been shouting bloody murder all day.

"Get my bandages and the mercury along with some opium," Doctor Commons demands, pointing at his medicine cabinet.

Running over to the glass door, I reach inside, pulling out everything Doctor Commons called for. Curling his arms underneath Jonathan's pits, Doctor Commons heaves him onto his patients' bed.

"Hand me the opium," Doctor Commons says, propping Jonathan's head with a pillow. Taking the glass bottle from my hands, Doctor Commons pours the beady black powder into a liquid solution. After mixing it, he drizzles it onto Jonathan's tongue.

Swallowing, Jonathan lies there, waiting with bloodshot eyes for the pain to vanish. His pupils are nearly behind his face. Doctor Commons takes the bandages and mercury from my hands and creates another solution with the mercury to soak the bandages in. He demands me to fetch a small basin from his kitchen and to bring it to him right away. Sprinting to and from the kitchen, I hand him the first basin I found atop his eating table. An odd place for a basin, but there is no time to ask questions.

Preparing the solution in a long-necked flask, Doctor Commons quickly grabs the basin and pours a pitcher of water into it. Sighing deeply, Jonathan falls asleep. The drugs took their course upon his weary mind. Completing the solution, Doctor Commons steadily pours it into the basin of water. Mixing it with a whisk, he creates a rose color liquid and soaks the bandages in it. After a short few seconds, he pulls them out of the basin and wrings out the excess solution.

Handing the bandages over to me, he says, "Now the bandages must soak in the liquid some more. I am going to clean out the wound and sear it to cease the bleeding and prevent infection. Hang the bandages on the drying rack by my medicine cabinet, and do leave. What I am about to do will not be pretty." Hurrying back into his kitchen, Doctor Commons is gone.

Looking down at Jonathan, I notice beneath the blood is a rusty piece of metal. It looks almost like a piece of a chisel.

"I told you to skedaddle, now go!" Doctor Commons shouts, ripping the bandages out of my hand and pushing me out the door. Slamming it in my face, Doctor Commons locks me out.

Throbbing, my head cries in pain.

Feeling like my head is going to implode, I wonder down towards city-square, trying to clear my thoughts. The more thoughts I muse over, the more my head hurts.

I hear chanting. I've been walking for no longer than five minutes, and there's already a ruckus. I can never clear my head. Maybe it's my overly active curiosity that pains my head; that's most likely because I'm drawn to the clamoring crowd instead of being repelled.

"Truth! Truth! Truth!" the people chant.

Increasing my pace, I arrive at city-square with a mild headache. A large crowd of people stand before The Square, pumping their fists in the air while chanting the word "truth" over and over. Jonah stands before them with his mouth closed. He seems to be frowning. The people are believing his words are true, but on his corpulent face there remains a frown. Not a frown that belongs to a person attending the funeral of their lost father, but rather of a parent disappointed in his or her children. It's a subtle difference. Not wasting his breath to speak over the people, he remains silent. At the very front

73

of the mob is the blacksmith making enough noise to make up for Jonah's silence. The blacksmith hollers with a voice that carries farther than any bird can fly without a break. In his fist he pumps up and down what seems to be a broken chisel snapped off at the body.

Suddenly I remember Jonathan. In his head was a piece of rusted metal. Stepping closer towards the chanting crowd, I squint my eyes. The chisel seems to be rusted through and through; there is not anything shiny or metallic about it. Looking around, I spot no guards, no soldiers, no generals. There seems to be no one who is daring to get near the mob. Taking another step, I hear a crunch beneath my bare feet. Pulling back my foot, I spot a fragment of bone now broken into smaller pieces. Jumping back, I yelp. Blood stains cleave onto the cobblestones I stand on. I remember the dead guards from yesterday's mob. My headache worsens. Pounding, the sounds around me become tidal waves.

It's all too much. It hurts all too much.

Sprinting away, I don't look back; I just run. I run and run until I cannot run anymore, and I cry. I cry until my eyes have no more tears to give. Then I look at the sun as I kneel by The Pit in my nightgown covered in mud.

I hate death, yet that's all I see in my head. Dying guards. A crowd of savages. Death.

"Get out of my head!" I cry, but it doesn't. It doesn't.

Chapter 12

Arriving at Doctor Commons' office late at night, I see Jonathan sitting up straight on the bed.

"How do you feel?" I ask. The bandages wrap around his head so that all I can see is his eyes, nose, and mouth. Looking at me with bloodshot eyes drained of any life, he shakes his head. "What happened?" I ask, walking closer.

"Don't get too close," he mutters cracking his knuckles.

Stopping, I figure I'm far enough away so he can't reach me.

"I'm sorry. Just wanted—"

"It was those blasted lunatics! Those boneheaded rioters dumber than the back end of an ass, and that blacksmith Austin Puntions is the worst of them all."

"The one with the broken chisel?"

"Yes! He drove that bloody thing into my skull for doing my job!"

"What do you mean by that?"

Pausing, Jonathan slides his lips together before replying, "I was commanded to bring Jonah in for questioning. Austin wouldn't even let me touch him. As soon as I reached for Jonah, Austin broke that damn chisel off my head. This just makes everything worse."

"Everything? What do you mean everything?"

Looking at me with knitted eyebrows, he shakes his head, "Why do you care so much to ask? You want to know, boy? Want to know what will happen? Well. war is going to happen. Liberty is going to invade us sometime. General Damon is preparing forces as we speak."

"Liberty? I thought they were peaceful."

"Not after King Oscar sent a snitch into their kingdom and swindled them of thousands of gold coins. They'll liberate us, all right. They'll liberate our heads from our necks."

Biting his bottom lip, he claws the side of the bed, peeling off the thin layer of padding. Shavings of red leather cling to his nails. Walking inside, Doctor Commons holds in hand a glass of water.

"Hydrate yourself if you want your humors to be in balance," he says, reaching the glass out towards Jonathan.

Taking the cold glass in his hand, Jonathan swallows the water in one big gulp, then hands the glass back to Doctor Commons.

"Give me more," he murmurs.

"Of course," Doctor Commons replies, hurrying back into the kitchen.

Looking at me with glowering eyes, Jonathan says, "Maybe Jonah wasn't wrong. There is a beast coming."

A shiver crawls down my back. Jonah described The Beast almost like it was a king. Maybe it was the king of Liberty.

Swallowing the lump in my throat, I reply, "Impossible."

"Tell that to my bloody head," Jonathan mutters, scratching at the uncomfortable bandages.

"Are the soldiers ready for war?"

"They're being sent out soon."

"How soon?"

Glaring at me like a possessed mummy, he growls, "What do I look like to you? Some sort of walking book with all the answers to your pathetic questions? Enough!" Throwing his hands in the air, Jonathan shoves me aside, marching out the door. I grab the back of his armor, but he kicks me in my shins. Groaning, I let go.

Doctor Commons comes walking speedily from the kitchen with another glass of water, but is left scanning the room inquisitively.

"Where is Jonathan?" he asks.

I point outside, trying my best to hide my underlying feeling of responsibility for his abrupt departure. My eyes so easily reflect my guilt.

"His head is far too damaged for him to take a walk. I must stop him!" Doctor Commons shouts, tossing the glass of water into my hands and splashing some of it on my tunic before running out the door. I can hear him shout Jonathan's name. Loud cursing follows until there is a long pause of silence.

Leaning my ear up against the door, I listen for the sound of Jonathan or Doctor Commons. I cannot make out any words, but can only hear quiet mumbling which slowly increases into shouting. Jonathan sounds like he is fuming.

"You have no idea what I have been through!" I can hear Jonathan bellow.

"Please, just come inside," Doctor Commons pleads.

"I'm living in hell! In hell!"

"Please, calm down. Come inside. Allow me to get you another water."

"Damn your water! Damn this city! I'll take matters into my own hands. Oh God, hold this not against me!" A loud gurgling noise like someone is choking on marbles scratches at my ears, followed by the loud mournful cry of Doctor Commons.

"Jonathan! No! Jonathan!"

Bursting out the door, I turn around to where I hear Doctor Commons grieving. Lying on the street with a dagger through his throat up into his head is Jonathan. Blood streams out his unhinged mouth and open nostrils onto his bandages which soak in the fluid. The blank stare of death washes over his face, and for a moment I envision a cackling shadow cross his chest like a crazed joker.

"Jonathan! Why Jonathan?" Doctor Commons mourns, digging his face into Jonathan's chest. I stand there beneath the moonlight. A dreadful silence consumes me. People slowly creep out of their houses, but I don't care to notice what they are saying or even doing. I am far too consumed in my own horror to notice. Creeping back into Doctor Commons' office, I work my way up to my room and close the door. I remain silent. I lie my head on my pillow and remain utterly silent. More silent than the night.

* * *

Delivering a eulogy on behalf of Jonathan, King Oscar proceeds to acknowledge the stress of a soldier's life. Yet he also acknowledges the dishonor in suicide. He seems to go back and forth between the two, making his speech seem rather counterintuitive. Though it really doesn't matter since the crowd cares little about what the king has to say. They simply hang their heads. I'm not entirely sure why. Believing that the city is grieved by Jonathan's suicide would overlook their hatred towards guards, but acting like they do not have feelings would imply they're not human.
Maybe I'm overthinking.
Slouching over, I feel overly encumbered with sorrow. Jonathan died on my account. I provoked him, and now he will be buried in The Pit like any other person who commits suicide. Fighting back tears, I flog my own mind with words of anger and bitterness. I willingly take in the cup of bitter poison called self-blame.
Standing by my side, Doctor Commons tries to raise my spirits by saying, "He was under great stress, and his head injury just set him over the edge. It is not your fault."
I shake my head replying, "I feel like it is."
"No one is to blame except the hand of the perpetrator."

78

Shrugging, I remain silent. King Oscar drags his speech on. I can't help but wish he would just stop where he is at. He keeps going in a circle.

"Responsibility is a burden, and beneath a blanket of gray it can even appear to be a persecutor. A soldier lives and dies with never ceasing responsibility and continual burdens laid upon him. That is why we honor our soldiers," King Oscar declares, pausing then returning to his speech, "That excuses no actions of self-harm, especially the voluntary eradication of one's life."

Here he goes again.

"Get on with it!" shouts a disgruntled townsperson from amidst the crowd. I can't find who said it, but I can only imagine the distaste on his face.

Resting his hands on his hips, King Oscar sighs, "Such a rude interruption. Especially at the funeral of a fallen soldier."

"It's because of you, fool! When is Liberty coming?" asks a woman directly behind me.

Turning around, I notice right away how she looks just like Jonathan. Their faces seem almost identical. If it wasn't for her feminine curves, alabaster skin, and long flowing hair, I could have sworn she was Jonathan.

Coughing, King Oscar replies, "Enough. We are here for Jonathan."

"Liar! Why don't you bury him in The Pit already? I know that's where you're going to take him!" she shouts back.

"Please—"

"You killed my brother!"

"I—"

"I blame you!" cries the woman behind me, ripping out her hair and gnashing her teeth. A devil would seem more sophisticated than her at the moment. Marching out of the crowd, she runs off, balling. The crowd, raising their heads, seem to have awoken.

"Look what you have done!" cries a stranger.

"See what you're doing!" shouts another.

King Oscar, shaking, slowly steps down from The Square, leaving Jonathan's casket behind. The frontline of the crowd moves towards him, but guards quickly intercede, allowing King Oscar to ride off in his golden and ivory carriage. Continuing to scream at him, the crowd raises their fists. Doctor Commons grabs me and escorts me to his house, quickly leaving the screaming mob behind as I start to cry again.

Chapter 13

At night, I can no longer sleep. Nightmares berate me relentlessly. Staring down at me with serpent eyes are those who died. Those that I have witnessed their final breaths. No longer is sleep a friend, but rather it is an elusive enemy. Even if it wasn't for the spirit of death, I wouldn't sleep well. My jaw aches too much.

The morning comes burning my weary eyes. Rising from bed, I feel sores on my feet. Blisters outline my soft fleshy sole.

I've been running around too much.

"Some sort of black magic, I say," I hear Doctor Commons mumbling. Treading softly, I follow Doctor Commons' voice down the steps. I take my time. My head throbs. He sits inside his kitchen, drinking a small glass of wine. He wears his simple nightgown made of black silk. Staring at me with heavy eyes, he sighs.

"What's wrong?" I ask.

Shaking his head, he replies, "I went out to city-square to buy some vegetables only to realize the whole market place was abandoned because of a burnt corpse on The Square by Jonathan's coffin. Driven through the corpse's chest," Doctor Commons says with a shudder, "was a crude sign saying, 'Have mercy on us,' in crimson. I could have sworn it was blood."

"What does it mean?"

"The body was burnt to a crisp with its arms crossed and legs broken outward. I believe it was some sort of black magic or evil sacrament towards The Beast. What fools."

"Who was it?"

Shrugging, Doctor Commons replies, "I could not tell. It was burnt pass the phase of distinguishment."

Scratching my head, I sit down by Doctor Commons.

"That's awful," I sigh. It seems a rather empty statement, but that is all I can muster to say.

"Yes, it is," he says, sliding his hand up and down the glass his wine sits in. Under an unseen cloud of confusion, I shake my head. So much has been happening that I can't discern it all at once. There is just too much going on.

"I would think it would just be better to be consumed by The Beast than to blindly try to fight it," I whisper, laying my face on Doctor Commons' polished kitchen table.

"The only beasts around are those who are killing foolishly," grumbles Doctor Commons.

"What about Liberty?"

"That is a kingdom, not a beast. Besides, Liberty isn't known for genocide. If they defeat our army, they will make us an annexation to their kingdom, treating us as one of their own. Why fear that?"

"What about pride? Isn't our kingdom worth fighting for?"

"One full of lies and scandals? I'd say not. For years I tried to reason with King Oscar as we grew up together, but he was always an over-embellished fool, even at the University of Cambridge. He never took the right path, but only the one that looked right."

"What does that mean?"

Swatting the air, Doctor Commons say, "He's a lazy hypocrite." Setting his glass down on the table he continues, "I only hate to see these people destroy themselves."

"Why don't you do something about it?"

Growling, Doctor Commons grits his teeth, "I have spoken with King Oscar and other officials about our kingdom's state, but they are just a bunch of strutting peacocks without any sense of what they are dealing with. Won't surprise me to see them all killed." I have never seen such tenacity in Doctor Common's face before. Growing beet red, he quickly shoots around, stomping away from the kitchen.

Standing up, I take a step towards his room then pause. I should just leave. It is best to grant Doctor Commons his solitude when he is upset.

The streets are empty. Hardly a sound can be heard besides the soft whistling of the wind bouncing off the stone walls. Walking alongside the many townhouses on Doctor Commons' street, I soon hear hushed voices. Not those belonging to neighbors, but rather contentious brothers. The hushed barking comes from a tarnished stone building no bigger than Doctor Commons' place. Someone is enraged.

Peering inside a dusty window, I scan the room. The two drunks along with a big guard are huddled in a circle. Sitting down with no drink, the drunks cower. Their hands are placed near their faces. Raising his voice, the guard rips into them while marching back and forth. His face is sharp, and his voice is booming.

"I told you two boneheads to bury that whore! Now she's out in the middle of town!" shouts the guard, spitting in each of their faces.

"We did bury 'er," protests the taller drunk.

"He's right," says the other.

"Then why is she out there in the public?" asks the guard.

"Some fellow must of moved 'er," replies the taller drunk.

"From The Pit?"

"Yes."

"Show me," the guard demands, spinning around. His gaze slides across my window. Flaring up, I quickly duck down. My heart beats rapidly. I feel something like that of a rock get caught in my throat. I struggle to breathe.

Stay calm.

Sneaking around the corner of the building, I hear the door slam shut. Crouching near the ground in between two houses that smell rotten, I wait with sweat beading around my brow. Heavy footsteps proceed up the street. Three pairs of feet enter my peripheral. Looking up at their faces, I hold my breath. If I'm caught, I don't know if even my name could save me. Walking quickly by me, they hurry for The Pit. Catching my breath, I wait a few minutes before crawling out from my hiding spot. The guard and the two drunks are nowhere to be seen. Still sweating, I look up and down the street.

Is the prostitute still at The Pit?

My fear demands I stand still, but my curiosity overcomes me. It's my demon inside. Stalking up the street, I shift my eyes every which way to make sure no one is watching me. After a few moments, I can see The Pit. The two drunks stand before the guard, pointing at a hole in the stony soil. Creeping behind the nearest tree, I peer around its trunk.

What is happening?

"We laid 'er there," says the taller drunk.

"Ain't no dead strumpet come trumping out 'ere," says the shorter drunk.

"Of course, not you bonehead!" shouts the taller drunk, hitting the shorter one over the head, "She dead."

"Knock it off! You two are disgraces to society!" bellows the guard, jabbing a finger at both of them.

"Sorry—"

"Don't apologize. Now someone saw you bury her. Who could it have been?"

Lost for words, the taller drunk doesn't know how to respond.

"Ain't no one I know. Maybe a witch," says the shorter drunk.

"No, you fool," the guard barks. "There is not a single witch in this city. They were all purged years ago."

"Maybe they coming back with The Beast and all."

"There is no beast."

"Tell that to them."

"If there is some sort of occult going on, it will be eliminated."

"A colt? Why colt for?" asks the taller drunk, scratching his chin.

"Never mind, you plebeian. Let me handle my business and you handle yours. Grab the corpse and bury her again."

"Yes, sir," both drunks reply, running awkwardly down the street. Standing stone still, the guard remains staring at the hole in the ground. His body is rigid like the thoughts he's musing over demand he be still.

"Damn those wretched town scum, they will pay with blood for what they are doing," he growls to himself. Turning around quickly, he looks at me. I slip behind the trunk of the tree as quick as I can, but I sense it was too late. Gasping for air, I glance left and right. I could run, but maybe he didn't see me. He had to see me! Yet I'm too scared to move. So, I sit still. I feel my face get hot and my blood run cold.

Breathe. Breathe.

Taking two deep breaths, I look around again. Nothing.

A few seconds go by, and I hear nothing. My breath steadies. I wait a few more seconds, and still nothing. My breath steadies some more. A few more seconds go by, and still nothing. Breathing normally, I wait a few more moments. Sighing, I roll out from behind the tree. A heavy foot drills me in my gut. Getting the wind knocked out of me, I hug my knees, grasping for a single breath, but I can't get even one.

"What have you heard?" asks the guard, baring his teeth.

Raising my hands, I inhale my first breath. My ribs ache and my lungs flare up.

"What have you heard?"

"Nothing," I lie in between deep breaths.

Grabbing me by my hair, he pulls me up to my feet. I shut my eyes groaning in pain. I know if I scream, he will beat me. Pausing, he analyzes my face.

"You're the son of High General Damon."

"Yes," I reply weakly.

"I best not harm you, but if you open your trap and tell others what you heard, I will skin you alive and feed your body to the crows. You understand?"

"Yes, sir."

Shoving me face first into the cobblestone, he spits on me before marching off where the drunks ran earlier. Scraped up, my face feels like someone scrubbed a bristly brush across my cheek. Lying still for a few minutes, I curse to myself. Then moaning, I stand up. My joints cry out in pain, popping back into place. My jaw throbs.

I hate that guy, I think to myself as I glare holes into his back.

Limping down the street, I wade in self-pity. Mumbling obscenities, I kick stones against neighboring houses. They ricochet off the houses, bouncing this way and that. I just imagine it's the guard's head.

Scuffling. My ears perk. I hear something like gravel against stone scrape together to my left.

Looking over, I spot a hooded figure lurking in the shadow of an abandoned house near The Pit. This area is normally avoided by people. Abandoned houses aren't uncommon. This guy, however, is. Propping one foot up against the wall and leaning his back against the crumbling stone, the hooded man seems to be angling his head towards me. My mouth dries like a desert. Walking slower, I stare at the hooded man. A black bag disguises his face, and he's covered in a black robe. Inching forward, I nearly stop when I'm only a few paces away from the mysterious man. All I can see of him are his meaty hands grasping his crossed arms. Coming to a halt, I stare at him, afraid if I look away that he might try to kill me.

Silence. Dead silence.

"He hurt you, didn't he?" the mysterious man asks with a voice so deep and gruff I can barely understand him.

Nodding my head, I continue to stare.

"Those weasels are monsters. Aren't they?"

I shrug.

Lowering his foot, he says, "Don't worry. They won't always hurt you."

I remain silent.

"They won't bother you. Soon enough, they won't bother anyone."

The mysterious man chuckles, shaking the bag over his head. I say nothing.

"Don't be frightened. I'm on your side. We're all on your side," he chuckles, pulling out a dagger from his robe. "Unity sometimes requires rebellion. Peace sometimes requires war. Freedom sometimes requires slavery. Those guards will soon know that fact as they drink their blood." Slicing his finger with the silvery dagger, he watches the blood ooze out. Sliding the bloody finger across his chest, he makes a crimson eye. Looking up at me through his sable bag, he whispers, "Beware The Beast." Then slinks away beneath the shadows.

Beware The Beast? What's going on?

On the ground, I notice a piece of paper. Picking it up, I flatten it out with my hands.

The night is our home.
The day is our hope.
Today is theirs.
Tomorrow will be ours.
Slay all who oppose.
And love those who don't.

Beware The Beast

Clenching the letter, I gaze into the shadows.
What's going on?

Chapter 14

"These sacrifices mean nothing to The Beast!" shouts Jonah over the ranting crowd.

"I heard him call my name! I heard him!" cries the woman with beautiful black hair. She stands inches apart from Austin Puntions. As the crowd thickens, she wraps herself around him.

"I saw a shadowy figure out my window slink by! It was The Beast, I swear!" cries someone else from the dense crowd.

As usual, I stand on the outskirts of the gathering. No need to get myself caught in the middle of a feud.

"Do you not understand what I am saying? You are all making hasty assumptions," Jonah protests, but no one seems to listen. He is their figurehead, not their leader.

"What are we to do about this all?" asks a sensible woman who stands not so far in front of me. Clothed in a common linen dress, she does not scream or shove her weight around, but instead simply raises her hand. Somehow, she was able to attract the attention of the crowd.

"I say we form a pact against this beastly creature and fight!" shouts Austin, pumping his fist in the air. The woman with beautiful black hair nods in agreement, laying her hand on his brawny chest.

"How are we to fight it?" the sensible woman asks.

"With blood."

"You can't be serious."

"He is not," Jonah protests. "You treat The Beast as a rat or some sort of pest that can be simply eradicated through mere force or poison, but he is like a venomous snake. He coils in the corner of every city street just waiting to be stepped on. Then he strikes with mighty force till every person is infected with his deadly venom. You must seek him out and be wise. Fools will only suffer more, and without prayer, the faithless will only perish."

"Then we seek him out. Tonight, we gather together and torch any sign of The Beast! He hides in the darkness. We must seek him out," Austin says. Cheering, the crowd agrees.

"There will be none of that!" bellows someone from behind me. Turning around, I notice my father on his stallion with a militia of men behind him. "If anyone is caught out on the streets at night, he or she will be killed on the spot. I have given every guard and every soldier the go to do so. Increased protection at night will guarantee the end to your scandalous schemes."

"That is tyranny!" cries Austin.

"Yeah!" chimes in the woman with beautiful black hair.

"It is only sensible," replies my father without any sign of pity on his face.

"You're a dimwitted jackass! You can't tell us what to do," Austin replies.

Nodding his head towards the mob, my father watches the soldier closest to him walk up to the man nearest to me. The man is fuming, cursing my father. The guard marches his way slowly. The fuming man continues to curse, raising his voice louder. Facing each other, the fuming man and the soldier look at each other briefly. With a sword by his side, the soldier impales the fuming man in the gut and twists his sword, squeezing blood out of the man's body like a sponge. People scream, and those closest to me rush the soldier but are all quickly stabbed by spears in the hands of the other soldiers on the front lines. The crowd screams still pushing forward, but as soon as a dozen people drop, including one woman, they begin to flee.

"This is not over!" Austin bellows, running off with the beautiful black-haired woman in his arms.

Bodies surround me. Several of them. Not all are dead. Many of them moan in pain, holding their sides or clenching their arms.

"Take them out of their misery," my father snarls, stepping down from his horse. Doing as commanded, a dozen soldiers pull out their sharp daggers, slicing the necks of the wounded. Many of the wounded cry for mercy, but a few remain silent. Only one continues to fume at the mouth, and it is the remaining woman. Aged with gray hair, she curses the guards till her last breath is drawn. With tears in my eyes, I fight the urge to weep.

Grabbing my shoulder, my father spins me around so that I face him. Looking into my eyes he says, "Do not cry over them. They are only troublemakers out to assuage their blood lust."

"Then why are they the ones dead?" I ask with little strength in my voice like I'm going to sob right here and now.

"I cannot wait till they burn down the city to take action. I must stop them now."

"What is this madness?" I look around my feet. A cold hand rests by my left ankle, it belongs to the first one killed by the sword.

"You better not side with them," he growls, clenching the nape of my neck with his sturdy right hand.

I don't reply. Slapping me over the head, my father drags me over to a soldier who towers above me.

"Take him to my home and watch him till I get back."

The soldier nods, taking hold of my arm. Yanking me along, he doesn't let me dawdle all the way to my father's home. Once there, he stands at the door not moving a finger. All I can do is lie on my bed and sleep.

Sleep away all my problems and pray that some sort of peace can come between the soldiers and the people.

Chapter 15

"Church is canceled," my father tells me at the table as we eat bacon, ham, and eggs for breakfast.

"OK. Why?" I ask. I only woke up a few minutes ago and am indifferent towards the world.

"The church elders along with the priest are meeting with the Royal Union."

Perking up, I look up from my silver plate to ask, "For what reason?"

Finishing his plate, he kicks back on his chair, sighing, "That is none of your business."

"So, you know?"

Sitting up straight, he glares across the table at me, "That is none of your business. Now drop the subject."

Biting my lip, I nearly ask why he brought up the subject in the first place if it was none of my business, but I restrain myself.

Relaxing, my father's muscles contract and no longer push out his leather tunic.

"I will be with the king this afternoon following the meeting. Keep your nose clean and stay away from city-square. This is no longer a safe city."

"Why does no one assassinate Jonah?" I don't want Jonah to be killed, but if they are so worried about the people starting a revolution, why not simply eradicate the leader?

Scratching his head, my father replies, "It is not that simple. Let us assume that we would embark on killing that lunatic. First, we would need to find him when

93

no one is around. If he dies in front of everyone, then we definitely have an uprising on our hands which could lead to civil war," pausing, my father takes a breath, "However killing him in private is nearly impossible since he is very allusive, and we suspect he is under constant protection by Austin at this point. Beyond all these obstacles, there is no guarantee that killing him will pacify the people. It could just make them even more furious. A dead leader can easily become a motivational martyr."

Nodding my head, I muse over how little I know. As a general, you got to look at all sides of an issue, not only one.

"What does the throne intend to do then?" I ask, pushing my plate aside.

Glaring at me again, he whispers, "Understand this. What is about to come is and will never be your business. Any action the throne takes will be just and under the truest concern for its people. The kingdom is under bondage and must be freed from this lunatic."

Freezing, I muster up the strength to ask, "How many must die for freedom?"

Gritting his teeth, he replies, "As many as necessary."

"That seems morally shallow."

"Shut your damn mouth!"

"Why? Are you going to kill me, too?" I snap back without thinking.

Yelling, he rips his steak knife out from his hand and thrusts it at my head. Diving to the side, I can see it fly by and stick into a crack between two stones. Sprawled across the ground, I look at my father, wide-eyed with fear. Like a mad man realizing how truly crazy he is, my father shakes his head.

"Get out," he whispers as he cradles his face with his scabrous hands.

I don't move. I can't move.

"Get out," he growls still holding his face. I notice the tips of his ears burn red, and one drop of blood slides out from under his hand.

Slowly rising to my feet, I creep towards the door like a hunter trying to sneak by a sleeping bear.

"Get out!" he screams, gnashing his teeth at me. His face burns like a wildfire and his eyes blaze with flames. Trickling down the corner of his mouth are small drops of blood. His nostrils are flared, and everything about him reminds me of the Devil.

"Get out!" he hollers one more time, cracking his hand against my back as I run outside. Slamming the door behind me, my father curses loudly.

Walking away from my father's house, I come across two lieutenants in their gold armor with several medals on their silver trimmed sashes acting like they saw nothing. Of course, they'll ignore what just happened. Speaking against my father would be handing my father their heads on a silver platter.

Getting closer, I notice a new emblem on their sashes. I know all the badges. My father taught me growing up what each badge was and what it stood for. However, this new emblem I never saw before. Both lieutenants are wearing diamond badges as dark as the night sky with a white skull in the center. Disregarding me, they walk by with their heads high, but beneath their hairlines I notice a dew of sweat.

A chill runs down my back. There is so much I don't know, and it scares me.

Hurrying outside The Manor towards Doctor Commons' house, I can see from the rise a small circle of people huddling outside Doctor Commons' place. Running down the stony path, I quickly come within close proximity of the group. So as not to draw attention to myself, I stroll along the roadway with my hands by my side. Chattering among themselves, the circle of people seems to have no interest in me. Nearing the group, I prepare to cut in between them so to reach Doctor

Commons' office. However, before I could react, the guy I was approaching from behind to pass beside usurps me by both my arms. He's wearing a raggedy top along with farmer trousers made from sackcloth. His gut sticks out far and his arms are filled with girth. With impeccable strength, he holds me as the others circle me. It's like I was swallowed by the group. Kicking, I cry out for help until a man wearing a jester's mask slaps me across the face.

"Quit jabbering you drunken blue jay. Now listen to me. What you know about this meeting?" the man in the jester's mask asks. The joker seems to be crying, but a superficial red smile makes him look creepily happy. A sadistic joker knowing his actions are wrong, but he finds pleasure in them.

"I know nothing," I snap back. A great deal of pain breaks across the back of my head like a tree fell onto my neck. Unable to turn around, I can only imagine someone with a giant rod is ready to beat me for every wrong answer I give.

"Don't lie to us," the jester whispers, "unless you want your head looking like a warped piece of lumber." Clicking his fingers, he chuckles menacingly then, grabbing me by the collar, growls, "Now, son of Damon, what in bloody hell is going on in that church?"

Spitting up bloody saliva, I whisper with much contempt, "My father tells me nothing. You have a better chance finding answers up an ass's back end than from me."

Am I a fool or a brave man?

"Beat him," the jester growls, backing into the circle. Throwing me onto my stomach, the man who held me earlier now props his foot on my back. Squirming, I feel weak like a bug beneath the boot of a knight. Neck-breaking pain shoots up my back. A rod at least the size of a trunk belonging to a juniper tree beats my spine. Another blow follows from what feels like a horse whip. Biting my bottom lip, I fight back tears.

Do not cower.

Several blows follow. They tear holes in my tunic. They tear holes in my flesh. They tear holes into my mind. I feel mentally weak. I'm on the verge of tears.

"Hey, you, over there! Stop what you are doing!" shouts a gravelly voice. Freezing, the circle of miscreants around me look down the street in fear. Fleeing, they scatter in several directions. I feel like I can breathe again, but soon I feel woozy. The world fades into a blur as a pair of tan boots runs up beside me. I feel a wave of blood crash against my skull as my eyes roll back into my head.

Chapter 16

Opening an eye, I notice Doctor Commons sitting on his stool with his chin resting on the palms of his hands. His eyes are closed, but I can tell he was crying not too long ago. The bags beneath his eyes are pink and his hair is a mess hanging in his eyes. His glasses are on his medicine table by his side. Groaning, I shift my weight off my ribs.

"Tommy," Doctor Commons says like he just woke from a dream.

"Yeah," I moan.

"Tommy, what happened?" he asks.

"Yes, what did occur?" a deep gravelly voice asks as well.

Lifting my head gingerly, I notice through my dewy eyes a large figure dressed in armor like what Chief Myles use to wear. Hanging down from his face is a thick black beard. Maybe he is the new chief of the guards.

"Who are you?" I ask hoarsely.

"I'm the guard who helped save your life."

No wonder they fled. This guy is massive, I think to myself.

"Thank you then," I reply weakly.

"Enough with the niceties, what happened?"

"He just woke up you cannot expect him to—" Dr. Commons says.

"Shut your damn mouth, we are facing a potential civil war. I have no time for trivial horse shit! What happened?" the large guard shouts, interrupting Doctor

Commons who still stands by my side with his one hand pressed against my back and the other on my chest, helping me sit up.

Stuttering I fail to respond.

"Goddammit, you had all night to sleep on it. Now tell me, you plebeian."

"He is no plebeian. He is the son of the High General Damon," Doctor Commons protests.

"I do not care," the guard replies, grabbing the end of my bed. "Tell me what happened."

Pausing, I take in a deep breath before replying, "They wanted to know—"

"Who is 'they'?"

"Whoever they were," I snap back. "As I was saying, those fellows took it into their hands to figure out what was going on in the church. They thought I would know because I'm the son of Damon."

"Did you?"

"No, that is why they cudgeled me."

"What else happened?"

"That is all I can recall."

Shaking the end of my bed, he growls, "Don't cut me short, you little plebeian bastard."

"I'm not. If you did not notice, sir, I was knocked out by those hooligans."

"Fine then, I'll be going," he says, lifting himself up, shaking my bed like there was an earthquake occurring. Before opening the door, he turns to face me saying, "If I find out you held information from me, I will feed your flesh to the birds, you little bastard."

As soon as he leaves, Doctor Commons shakes his head, whispering, "What a despicable character he is."

"Who was that fellow, and what was his deal?" I ask, resting my head back down so that all I see is the wooden ceiling. I feel lightheaded sitting up.

"He is the new chief of the guards. He finds it to be his sole mission in life to end this revolution."

100

"I don't remember a formal introduction at The Square."

"King Oscar wanted it to be on the down low, I suppose. Do you need anything to drink or eat?" Doctor Commons asks.

"I am a little parched," I reply.

I hear Dr. Commons scuttle into the kitchen. Arriving quickly with a glass of water, he helps me sit up to drink it. The water is very refreshing as it slides down my throat. My mind seems to clear.

"Thank you," I say after I finish drinking.

"You're very welcome," he responds, going back into the kitchen.

I rest my head back down, and before I know it, I fall asleep.

* * *

Awakening, I notice darkness has taken over. I can hear Doctor Commons snoring from his bedroom.

What time is it? I think to myself as I sit up. A cold hand wraps around my mouth as an arm creeps around my waist holding me tight. I can feel someone's warm, sticky breath on my neck. Tremoring, I can hear my heart bang against my chest. My eyes widen with fear and my palms become slicker than fishes from the sea.

"Do not scream. I am here to help," whispers a dark, ominous voice. It is the same voice that belonged to the hooded man in black. The one who painted a bloody eye on his cloak. "I got word that a couple angry men are out for your blood. I do not know who, but if my sources are correct, they will be here any moment. Now I am going to release your mouth. Do not say a word." Letting go of my mouth, he waits behind me to see if I will make a noise. I don't dare. If I do, Doctor Commons will get himself killed. Satisfied, the man dressed in all black creeps by the door. Wearing what he wore when we first met, he stands up straight with his back up against the

101

wall. Pulling out a dagger from his waist, he stands there, not making a sound. He looks like a simple shadow blending in with the darkness. Excruciating minutes slip by as we both wait to see if what he said is true.

The door knob turns. The door creaks open. Moonlight breaks into Doctor Commons' office. Two men, one being the giant guy who held me as I was beaten, stand at the door with jester masks on and common clothing that farmers wear. In hand, the giant guy holds an axe as the scrawnier fellow has a club. Taking a couple steps forward, they reach the office floor. Swinging his arm around like lightning, the cloaked man shoves his dagger through the throat of the large guy. Taking his other hand, the cloaked man wraps his hand around the throat of the smaller fellow. Falling instantly, the giant guy collapses outside, but the scrawny fellow scrapes at the arm of the cloaked man who has him above the ground. Taking his now bloody dagger, the cloaked man lets go of the scrawny fellow's throat for a split second to thrust the dagger through his jugular. He too collapses quietly outside. The only thing breaking the silence are the snores of Doctor Commons.

Before I can even blink, two other shadowy figures carry the two dead bodies away.

"Do not tell anyone about this," whispers the cloaked man as he slinks outside, shutting the door.

Darkness consumes my vision. Scanning the room, I wait for more shadowy figures, but none appear. Lying back down, I stare at the ceiling, dumbstruck.

Why am I such a target? Why do I have to be a son to a general?

Cursing underneath my breath, I push aside the urge to go outside and find that shadow fellow. The one that wears that odd cloak. I push aside the urge to ask him the million questions on my mind. Instead I close my eyes.

The clock strikes midnight.

Chapter 17

"Come with me, Tommy," Doctor Commons says, dragging me outside.

I just woke up not so long ago and barely had time to eat my porridge. Wearing a simple tunic which has frayed ends and scratches my neck, I follow Doctor Commons outside. There is a meeting at city-square. The church along with a representative of the throne are calling the city together to address the potential uprising. I can already imagine the man in the black cloak is going to be there in some way. I fear that the meeting may turn into a bloodbath in a blink of an eye. Arriving at city-square, Doctor Commons and I are forced into the center of the multitude by the dozens of guards condensing the crowd.

"Move it! Everyone move in!" shouts the guard shoving Doctor Commons and I past the wall of disgruntled commoners.

Doctor Commons never releases my arm. My hand is so white from how hard he holds me. Falling farther into the sinkhole of people, I realize there are hundreds of guards surrounding the crowd, on the watchtowers, even on top of buildings. The guards on the watchtowers, which are spaced evenly on the wall surrounding our city, watch the crowd with eagle eyes ready to strike at any moment with their bows. Marching across the top of residential buildings, some of the guards carry pomegranate-shaped iron balls. I never saw them before, but the guards carrying the iron balls are also carrying torches. A chill runs down my back.

"If I did not know better, I could swear we are walking into a massacre," Doctor Commons whispers to me, his bottom lip quivering.

Hundreds of people fill the already dense city-square crowd. Shoulder to shoulder, the crowd stands with barely enough space for our chests to rise and fall so that we can breathe. Rising onto The Square, a noble looking man in a strange looking coat and baggy trousers with golden trim raises his hands in the air. Some of the nobles are trying to impose a new style, or maybe they just want to flaunt their superiority.

"Silence!" he shouts with a voice reminding me of a boy going through puberty. His face is plump, and his stomach is round. Still whispering among themselves, the crowd ignores him.

"Silence!" he shouts again, but still nobody listens. Pointing at a guard to his left, the nobleman nods.

A guard, carrying one of those pomegranate iron balls, lights the wick. Throwing it in the air, towards an empty street, the guard steps back. I watch, wondering what it will do.

A terrible explosion throttles my ears.

A fireball sends metal scraps flying into the surrounding buildings. The crowd gasps in horror.

"I said silence. Now are you listening? Next time, one of those grenades will be heading for city-square instead of a vacant street," the nobleman says callously.

Silence. Not even a baby can be heard crying.

"Good. Today we have gathered together to discuss the potential civil war you people are developing. King Oscar himself was not able to come because the discourse in this city made it far too dangerous for him to deliver this speech himself. This is unacceptable! You hear? Unacceptable! These city walls, they protect you. These guards, they defend you. These homes, they give you shelter. If you start a war, this will all be taken away."

104

"Liberty will do that for us!" shouts a brave man.

I cannot see him through the thick horde of people, but I can only imagine that he looks like a drunk.

"We have soldiers out in battle to defeat Liberty. Our army is currently winning. You raise fears that have no reason to be raised. You create tensions that should not even exist. You are destroying yourselves. King Oscar is trying to protect you, and like children, you retaliate."

"You call this protection?" asks the same man.

I still can't see him, but his voice is exactly the same — shaky and scared. And a little angry.

"You cannot see the full picture. King Oscar knows what is best for everyone here."

"This is going to solve nothing," Doctor Commons whispers in my ear.

"The church gives its full support as well. Father John, please speak to your children," says the nobleman.

Rising from his stool, Father John joins the representative on The Square. Wearing his priestly clothing along with his giant cross necklace, Father John looks older than usual, as if this is not an option, but rather a duty, to speak publicly. Gazing down at the bottom of his white robe, Father John sighs. Raising his head, he scans the multitude before him with sunken eyes that look like they belong to a dead person.

Then finally, clearing his throat, he speaks, "God's people are meant to be united as one body. The arms are to work with the body as the body is to work with the arms. The legs are to work with the body as the body works with the legs. Now such discourse among brethren divides the body. Instead of working as a body of believers, division makes a body of believers into backstabbers," pausing Father John swallows a lump in his throat, then proceeds, "and these backstabbers then plunge their blade not only into their own body, but into the entire church. King Oscar is also aware that the city is heading towards damnation unless repentance occurs and there is union once again."

Suddenly, many people begin screaming at Father John. Some call him a traitor and others a blasphemer.

"Father John along with the rest of the church gives its full support!" Father John's cry can barely be heard over the uproar.

"You are just a puppet! A puppet in the hands of the king!" cries the woman beside me. Looking over, I see it is the woman with beautiful black hair. Fresh scars caress her cheeks and bruises discolor her neck. Anger seems to be coursing through her blood, but sorrow seems to reside in her watery eyes. Austin stands next to her with a bulky arm around her neck. Bellowing, he swears uncontrollably. The lady with beautiful black hair trembles whenever his arm moves, but when Austin relaxes, she does the same. It is like their connected.

The uproar swallows Father John's voice. I watch his mouth move but hear nothing. Looking up, I spot a guard bringing his torch down towards his grenade. He throws it in the air.

It's coming for us!

"Run! Run!" I cry, shoving my elbow into Doctor Commons' side so that his grip loosens on my wrist. Then grabbing his arm, I try to pull him with me, but it's too late. A massive explosion shakes the ground. Shoving Doctor Commons onto the ground, I lay over top of him with my arms wrapped around him. A blaze of fire lights up behind us as screams of peril encroach on my ears. Tears fill my eyes as the heat nips at my heels and metal shrapnel scatters. Sobbing, I cannot hear a thing. A ringing noise deafens me. Feet rush by and a stampede of people run into each other. Embracing Doctor Commons, I weep. Swimming through tears, my eyes find Doctor Commons' face. His eyes remain shut. I cry out his name, or so I think. I still can't hear anything.

A pair of arms carry me away. Kicking and screaming, I cry out for Doctor Commons, but he continues to stray farther away.

"Doctor Commons!" I cry in between sobs. My eyes drown again in another pool of tears. A heavy club hits me behind the head, and my eyes choke on water. Dark, murky water.

* * *

"What were you thinking?"

"I gave my men an order. Not to kill."

"Then why are there dead civilians out there?"

"Because someone broke that order!"

"You know what this means? You know what any of this means? We have a potential war on our hands not only with Liberty, but our own people!"

Creeping out of my father's bed, I stalk towards the bedroom door.

"I realize that, King Oscar," I hear my father say.

"You are going to get us all killed!" shouts King Oscar.

"My men can handle it."

"Like they handled that crowd today?"

"We will beat them, hang them, and scare them to death so that they don't even think about rebellion!"

"That is a great idea," King Oscar says sarcastically. "Why don't you also sleep with another prostitute and drink some mead as our kingdom is swarmed with angry commoners?

"We have no other choice."

"Because of you. If you do not handle this situation in ten days, I am going to find myself a new general."

The house shakes as the door slams shut. Grabbing the back of my head, I feel a jolt of pain shoot down my neck. A lump bigger than my elbow rests beneath my fingers. Marching towards my room, my father's shadow forebodes at my door. Jumping back into bed, I hear the door creak open.

"Get your ass into the kitchen and eat," he says somberly.

Walking slowly into the kitchen, I notice a bowl of what looks like mush waiting for me. Sitting down at the table, I force myself to swallow the thick mush which tastes like waste from out back. Taking another bite, I see a splinter at the edge of the table. Like a piece of metal struck it from one of those—

Doctor Commons!

Throwing my spoon onto the floor, I kick back my chair heading for the door, but a hand grabs me by the shoulder, spinning me around.

"Where are you going?" asks my father with a snarl. His canines stick out like a rabid dog.

"What happened to Doctor Commons?" I ask.

"He is fine for now."

"For now?"

A horn bellows over The Manor.

"I am going to murder some bloody person," my father growls.

"What was that?" I ask.

Swirling his glass of rum, my father looks out the nearest window with an empty stare. Moving his lips, he tastes every drop of his last sip before he swallows. Resting his half-full glass on the table, he breathes in and out so that his scruff dances.

Setting his lips, he replies, "That, Thomas, is the sound of judgement."

Chapter 18

Sitting at my father's table, I stare at the door. My father left without any other words to share with me besides the same phrase, "Stay here."

The clock struck midnight not so long ago, and I stare at the door.

Doctor Commons.

I can still hear my father in my head. I still hear him reassuring me Doctor Commons is perfectly fine; for now. Scratching the table, I bump against my father's glass of rum. Taking hold of the glass, I bring it to my lips. The pungent smell of alcohol makes my nostrils curl in with disgust, but I take a swallow. It hits me like an arrow to the chest. Coughing, I spit it back up. It is disgusting. Turning around, I wipe my mouth.

A chill runs down my back.

I am not alone.

Turning towards the door, I see that it is open. The cold night air chills the room. Standing up, I look around, but all I see is darkness. Yet more than darkness is here. I can feel it. It's like I have a sixth sense.

"Who is there?" I whisper. Backing towards the door, I spot a shadow scurry across the wall. Jumping out of my chest, my heart tears away at my ribcage.

Breathe, Thomas. Breathe, I think to myself, but it does no good.

Grazing the door, I shut it. The walls groan and the wind outside whistles. They are playing a serenade for me before I die. Stalking forward, I inch towards my room.

The stairs moan. Gasping, I swing my head around. Sweat trickles down my back. Skulking, I rub my fingers against the stairs. Another icy chill freezes my spine

"Who is there?" I whisper. Silence follows.

Run. Just run, Thomas.

Swallowing, I back away from the stairs. Letting out a heavy breath, I turn around. The door is only a few steps away. A ray of light dances across it. Freezing, I feel someone's warm breath on the nape of my swollen neck. A candle flickers on the edge of my peripheral, and someone's hand rests on my shoulder. A tear leaks from the corner of my eye.

"Do not cry, my child. It is only I," the voice whispers. Turning around, I see that it is the hooded man. A sinister chuckle escapes his mouth, "A cruel trick I played. I realize that, but I certainly found enjoyment in it."

"What do you want from me?" I ask.

Chuckling again, he pats my shoulder. The candle's glow flirts with his hood, cavorting like a strumpet.

"I only need to know what your father told you."

"What do you mean?"

Laughing, he shakes his hood.

"Don't play coy with me. You certainly heard his plans with our little city. He certainly is not a silent one."

"He told me nothing."

"Do not lie to me, child."

"I am not."

"What did he say?"

"Nothing."

Usurping my neck, the hooded man squeezes me so hard I can feel a blood vessel burst.

"No more games, kid. For your own safety. For our entire damn kingdom, what did your father say? What did he say!?" he growls, shaking me like a twig.

"He promises torture," I cry.

Letting me go, he clenches a fist.

"What kind of torture?"

"I do not know. Hangings, floggings, maybe more. I do not know."

"That bastard," he snarls. "Listen to me. Your father is going to die. This entire kingdom is run by corrupt bastards."

"My father?"

Ripping off his mask, I can only see the left side of the hooded man's face for a second before he puts out his candle with his fingers.

"Feel my face, kid."

"What?"

"Feel it!" Grabbing my hand, he rubs my hand over his left cheek. Millions of scabs and scars mark his face. They feel like mountain ranges and vast plains with craters everywhere.

"That is your father's handiwork."

"What do you mean?"

Throwing down my hand, he replies, "Don't insult me with such questions. You are no fool. Listen to me. As I said before, I am on your side, but I do not have the patience for horse shit. Be honest with me, and I will be honest with you."

Rubbing my sore wrist, I reply, "Then tell me who you are."

Pausing, the cloaked man takes in a breath and covers himself once again with his hood.

"It is better that you don't know."

"Why should I trust you then?" I ask, my voice cracking. Bubbling inside with anger and confusion, I ball up my fists. There is no way I will swing a punch, but something inside me wants to very badly.

Leaning in towards my face, the cloaked man wraps his dry fingers around my chin.

"Because I am trying to save this goddamn kingdom. If you want to keep testing my patience, you can give up your soul to The Beast and be food for the crows because I can kill you quicker than any guard here." In a blink of an eye, he has me by the neck and his dagger pressed against my right cheek. Whispering in my ear, he says, "Beware The Beast." His arm tightens around my neck. I can feel my face begging for blood. I can feel my lungs imploding.

He's strangling me!

Kicking my legs against his, I squirm as much as I can, but he is not fazed. His strength is far greater than mine. Waning weaker, I slowly go limp. My vision blurs, and different colors speckle the darkness.

This is it, I think somberly.

Giving up, I let my body hang in his arms.

Rustling. There is rustling. Something. Something. Rustling. Something. Something. Rustling...

"Sleep."

* * *

Gasping, I shoot up. Panicked, I look every direction to only be surprised even more.

My legs are gone!

Wait. They're only lost beneath a giant blanket. Patting my surroundings, I feel wool. Glancing down at my hand, I notice my bed. I am in my father's home in my room. Getting up, I stare in disbelief at my bed. The pillows laced with silk, the bed's mattress clothed in the finest wool, and the blanket woven so perfectly that it could only belong to someone with prestige.

I cough. My throat feels raspy. The darkness around me has lessened but still lurks around. Walking out into the kitchen, I notice the door is shut. On the table is a note. Unfolding the small piece of paper, I only read three bold words.

BEWARE THE BEAST

Shoving the note in my tunic right by my chest, I run outside. Nobody gives me a second glance. Not a guard seems to acknowledge my presence; they all wear

112

black diamond badges with white skulls on them. Every guard, every soldier, every lieutenant has one. I bump into one guard as I run, and he doesn't even bother to look down at me. He keeps marching down the hallway we are in.

Doctor Commons did not escape my memory. Arriving at his door nearly out of breath and my throat cursing me for running so much, I trump inside. Glass is everywhere. His precious bottle of mercury is smashed into bits beneath his medicine cabinet. His bed for patients is shredded. Food is scattered everywhere. A kettle of porridge rests against the stairwell with gooey oats splattered up against the wall. It looks like a twister tore apart his office.

"Doctor Commons!" I call out his name, "Doctor Commons!"

"Up here, Tommy," whispers a meek voice from upstairs. Avoiding the piles of glass, I jump from space to space till I reach the steps and bolt upstairs. The door to my room remains open. Hurrying inside, I come to a halt. Doctor Commons sits on the edge of my bed with only a loincloth on.

"What happened?" I ask in shock. Never have I seen Doctor Commons in such a state. Staring out my window, he seems to be trapped in a dungeon. A self-made prison. Lost in his own despair. He looks empty.

"Are you referring to me or to the office?" he asks in a distant manner, like he is questioning a voice in his head rather than me. Afraid to get near him, I stand at the edge of the bed.

"Either one."

"What you see are the remnants of a broken spirit. What you saw were the remnants of my practice."

"That does not answer my question," I protest.

"Most certainly does, Tommy. That is what happened."

"Did you do this to yourself?"

"I should have seen it coming, I suppose. Those crazed lunatics certainly were bound to lose control."

Tightening his fist, Doctor Commons crumbles a piece of paper I haven't cared to notice. Stepping closer, I look at it and then pull out the note I have.

"Is that a note?" I ask.

Still looking out the window with a hollow stare, he nods.

"It was meant to be a warning, though his warning is almost worse than death."

"Who was it? Who did this?" I plead, grabbing Doctor Commons by the shoulder. Tears stream down my cheeks.

"It does not matter."

"Tell me!" I scream, shaking Doctor Commons. His body is like a corpse. Not resisting, he allows himself to be jerked back and forth without a care. He is cold to the touch.

"Don't fret over me. I will be fine," he whispers. Shimmering, his eyes glaze over with icy tears.

"Speak to me!" I holler before slapping Doctor Commons across the face with all my might. It stings my hand like a bee, but his face suffered more. A fiery red hand print marks his concave cheeks. Snapping around, he grabs me by my wrist. My hand remains where I slapped him.

"Don't let their spirit control you. Fight it. The Devil himself wants to devour your soul. Don't let him have it! You hear me!? Do not let him have it!" he shrieks, his throat constricting and his eyes bulging. His body convulses and his face turns three different shades of red. I try to pull back, but he holds on tighter to the point I feel like my wrist is going to snap, "Don't let him have it! You hear? You hear?!"

I slap him with my other hand. Tears now pour down from my face like waterfalls. Collapsing onto the ground, Doctor Commons weeps as he drops the note. Quickly bending over, I snatch it up, unfolding it rapidly.

I asked for help
You gave me none
So, enjoy living hell
When everything is gone

Crying, I rip the note apart, throwing the two halves onto the floor. Then falling onto my knees next to Doctor Commons I join him in his cry.

Chapter 19

Doctor Commons does not get up in the morning. He remains sleeping in his room, or so I assume. I do not dare to breach inside and disturb him if he is or isn't sleeping. His office, still in shambles, creates a maze of disaster for me to tiptoe around so that I can make myself some sort of breakfast. I find a few slices of bread here and there on the table and a cracked jar of strawberry preserves in the corner of the kitchen. Slathering the strawberry preserves over three slices of bread, I stack them on top of each other and eat them all at once. Going down into Doctor Commons' cellar, I find a musty bottle of watered-down beer to drink. Satisfied, I wipe my mouth, leaving the half empty bottle on the cellar floor. Doctor Commons remains in his room. Standing by his closed door, I feel the hopelessness seep out from beneath it.

I am unable to decipher how I feel. Maybe bitter, but enough bitterness consumes the city as is. Bitterness is far too overwhelming to indulge. Perhaps an underlying sense of oppression lives inside me. The cloaked man robbed me of my carefree life and stole from me my closest friend. My only true friend. Confused. Angry. Sad. Are all emotions I feel. Emotions I have felt over the past three weeks that have gone by. The city I live in is falling apart, and I can't help but feel like I am unfairly caught in the middle of it all.

Shaking my head, I leave Doctor Commons' office. I love him, but there is nothing I can do to help him. Last night, after our sobbing, he didn't even acknowledge my presence. He went mute, almost like he became someone else.

How can I help if he's silent? Or if I can't help myself? I hate feeling this way. I hate these questions.

Sliding my feet against the cobblestone path, I try to clear my head. If I could only die or be able to go back in time, then everything would be fine. The city-square, filled with many people, seems to be buzzing with excitement. Austin Puntions can be seen running around telling everyone Jonah, on this day, is going to deliver a speech.

"Jonah is coming! He is going to come at any moment! He has a message to share!" Austin exclaims to everyone. The joy on many faces cannot be hidden. Jonah has, overnight, swept the city off its feet and now carries them in his hands. If he would think murdering children was perfectly acceptable, all parents that day would sacrifice their children for his cause. Representing the common person, Jonah is a figurehead of freedom.

"Jonah is coming! Jonah is coming!" Austin shouts. He prances by me like a giddy child. A few cheers break out.

Turning towards The Square, I spot Jonah rising onto the platform before the gallows. Every person stops what they are doing and directs their attention towards Jonah. He never changes what he wears. He still wears a simple robe along with that golden ring of his.

"Greetings," he says. Many people cheer in response. Jonah does not smile. He does not even grin. Constructed in a serious manner, his face does not express any sense of joy. "I have come to speak to everyone once again."

"Thank you for doing so," Austin says from the crowd.

Nodding, Jonah continues, "It has come to my attention that many believe The Beast can be warded off

118

with black magic and murder. All these assumptions are false. Rather, he is the root of all that evil."

"Did you not say we are to seek out The Beast?" asks a man.

"What does this have to do with murder and black magic?" replies Jonah.

"Those who live with The Beast inside them must be dangerous and therefore killed."

"How many times do I have to remind you that The Beast is here in the spirit and not in the physical? Simply killing a man will not destroy The Beast as much as murdering a prostitute will not eliminate fornication."

"That is why black magic must be performed. To summon The Beast so we can kill it," says Austin.

"That is like calling upon the Devil so that you can murder him. There is no way on God's green earth that anyone of you can destroy The Beast on your own."

"So, we need an army."

"Yes, but not in the terms you speak."

"We need an army and we need resources that only King Oscar can provide."

"What do you speak of?" Jonah asks. Furrowing his eyebrows, he suspects the worst.

"Far too long King Oscar has been dictating our lives. For God's sake, I can't leave my home after nightfall without the threat of being killed by some weasel," Austin declares, pumping his fist in the air as the crowd cheers and applauds. "Today we demand his respect!" Everyone shouts, whistles, and claps in response.

"The Beast is a divider—"

"Then we'll take down the source of the division!" Austin proclaims, interrupting Jonah. Arousing the crowd, Austin jumps up onto The Square, throwing his arm around Jonah and shouting, "Together we will be stronger! We will slay The Beast, and we will regain our freedom!" Whooping can be heard from all directions. Even children are chiming in by clanking together pans or raising their pubescent voices so that they too are heard.

Lowering his head, Jonah slouches his shoulders, though no one seems to notice. Jonah speaks under conviction. Austin speaks with fire. Using Jonah's truthfulness to his advantage, Austin can so easily manipulate others for his own doing under the impression he is in alignment with Jonah. Jonah swept the people off their feet and into his hands, but Austin is the voice that they hear in their one-track revolutionary minds.

"First we must claim our territory! For now, on this side of the kingdom," Austin points in the opposite direction of The Manor, "is our side, and that side," he points toward The Manor, "is theirs."

Thwack!

An arrow lodges itself into the side of the gallows behind Austin. Spinning around, I notice guards have gotten into positions on their watch towers and several have gone into formation in front of the Gate House. More arrows fly overhead, and Austin dives out of the way, knocking Jonah over in the process. Two people in front of The Square collapse with arrows going through their chests. The line of guards in front of the Gate House make space down the center of their formation for the chief of the guards. His massive body makes those behind him look puny. With a battle axe thrown over his wide shoulder, he stares down the mob of people.

The arrows cease to fly, and the mob stops shouting.

"I heard you lay claim on your territory, but words and actions differ in results," the chief of the guards says. No one responds.

"If any dare to lay claim of their territory, come at your own risk; but I suggest everyone runs because whoever remains will be slaughtered."

There's a pause, a long, drawn out pause, until a single grenade crashes against the ground bursting into smoke; but it is not the mob that suffers. The guards do. Their formation crumbles, leading to a barrage of many

120

more grenades that fly from alleyways and house windows. Balls of fire and smoke light up the guards as they cry out in agony. Some flee. Others drop to the ground, scratching at their faces littered with metal bits. Shocked, the chief of the guards turns around to see his men falling over. They cry out in pain. Shrapnel is lodged deep into their flesh. The men, the hooded men, must finally be ceasing their opportunity for revolution.

"Charge!" Austin shouts.

Letting out a war cry, everyone rushes forward. Fighting to escape, I try to weave out of the mob, but I can't. Feet kick me, arms hit me, and if I'm not careful I will be trampled. So, joining the mob, I run in unison with their path. Arrows come raining down like hail. Many people are falling, but many more keep running. The chief of the guards, lowering his battle axe, swings with all his might, clobbering the first three people who get near him and decapitating the one. Swinging again, he strikes five more, but the crowd becomes too large to handle as an army of arms claw him down. I can hear him curse in between angry cries of pain as the mob rips him apart with nothing but their bare hands. The guards who survived the preliminary attack are quickly overrun. A ball of people lumps together and rams the Gate House door down. Funneling inside, the mob screams even louder as the arrows above dissipate. The guards on the wall are fleeing.

A screaming child sprints by me with a bloody arrow in hand. A hole in his shoulder oozing blood is a deep shade of red. Turning around, I see a gap in the crowd. A tunnel of hope to escape the mad men, women, and several children who are tearing down the Gate House. Sprinting through the gap, an arm clotheslines me, knocking me onto my back with a thud. Gasping for air, I feel like I am going to die. Hundreds of people run by, and some step on my legs, gut, and arms. Wincing, I can feel the tears welling up in my eyes. My head throbs and my jaw feels like it's going to crack.

I wasn't made for this.

Cold hands grab my ankles, pulling me to safety. Then jumping into my vision, I see a wiry fellow with teeth that stick out over his bottom lip like a troll.

"You all right, fellah? Mighty hard fall," he says, licking the blood off his lips. Pieces of flesh stick in between his front teeth, and the smell of death leaks from his mouth. Staring at his bloodshot eyes, I see that his pupils are smaller than the head of a needle.

"I'm fine," I manage to whisper. Sniffling, I wipe away a couple tears.

"Good. Now join us. Those weasels deserve what's coming," he cackles. Snorting, he licks his lips again.

"Go on without me," I say.

He nods.

"As you wish. I will eat off their pain." Laughing hysterically like a jester, he runs for the Gate House.

Rolling over, I feel my bones crack and my muscles strain. Pushing myself up, I hobble onto my feet. The Gate House, now filled with townspeople, is being looted of everything ranging from swords to gold. There are others on top of the wall whooping and hollering. Some hold up the heads of archers as others fire arrows towards the sun. On one of the outlook posts there is someone scanning the city. Then nearly jumping out of his skin he pulls out a horn and blows into it three times. The mob freezes for a second as if to think about what the signal means. Fleeing with swords, axes, arrows, and bows, hundreds of people run into the territory claimed by Austin earlier. It is now their territory.

We are a city divided.

Chapter 20

My father comes barreling in on his horse with a thousand men behind him ready for war, but once they arrive, everyone is gone. If my father would go into the other side of the kingdom as is, it would be a suicide mission. Highly weaponized and hiding in obscure places, the townspeople finally have the upper hand. Standing like a lone idiot in the middle of city-square, I cry. There is no warrior inside me.

"Why do I always spot you out here?" questions my father.

Turning around, I look at him with tear-filled eyes.

"What?" I ask.

"You are always out here when things go wrong. What incentive do you have for frolicking among the despicable?" he questions, bending at the knees so he is able to face me.

"I don't know," I blubber.

Swatting me over the head, he replies, "Use your head, you worthless mutt."

"What?"

Softening, my father whispers, "Ignore that, come with me." Reaching out for my shoulder, he gets closer.

I slap his hand, growling, "You are my incentive."

Running for the territory of the townspeople, I ignore the cries of my father behind me. Weaving through dark alley ways and shady lanes, I run. The streets are unfamiliar to me. The only pathway I know on the west side of the kingdom is the pathway to church. Otherwise,

I never travel through the west side. However, I can't stand the idea of being locked in my room to never be let out again until this civil dispute is over. Never being able to be with Doctor Commons, the real Doctor Commons. Not the depressed shadow in his spare room. I know that's exactly what my father had in store for me. He wants me trapped inside The Manor as long as possible. Finding the main road that passes through the west side, I bound down the lanes that I know lead to the chapel. The streets are stiffly silent, which is surprising. I would have thought that after such a successful attack the townspeople would be elated. On the other hand, they may be hiding or maybe waiting to see if my father has the guts to cross over and invade. Reaching the church, I spot Father John hanging a wooden cross over the main entrance of the chapel. Scratching his ear, he turns around weakly at the waist and smiles warmly.

"I thought I heard footsteps," he says raspy. Panting, I shrug. Frowning, he wraps his arm around my shoulders. "Come with me, son. You look like you need a place to stay." Leading me up the stairs to the chapel's main entrance, Father John hums a hymn.

"I am sorry to disturb you," I say after I have regained my breath.

"You have not disturbed me, my child. Rather your company is much appreciated. Not many have come by the church as of late, and it can get awfully lonely around here," he replies.

Walking down the center of the sanctuary, Father John guides me to a door located behind the pulpit. The door is located at the bottom of five steps; it's concealed from sight if you sit inside the sanctuary. Behind the door is a long corridor with many bible verses painted on the walls in black ink. Gold trimming laces the hallway and polished marble makes up the floor. At the end of the corridor is a round room that is filled with many books. There are shelves full of them. A chandelier dangles from the ceiling, illuminating the room. Taking a right, Father

John leads me to another room that is much smaller than the others and is made mostly out of marble. At the opposite end of the door is a rectangular cut out in the marble floor that is longer than my body from head to toe and wider as well. At the edge of the cut out are many ointments, oils, and bars of off-yellow soap.

"You look like you haven't cleaned yourself properly in a long time. Take a bath, my child, and then when you are finished, I will have food prepared for you," Father John says. Closing the door, he leaves me alone.

A black wool robe hangs on the wall by the bath house's door. Not hesitating, I quickly strip down and run towards the tub with an actual smile but find the tub to be empty. Assuming there is a mistake, I prepare to ask Father John where water can be found to fill the tub, then to my surprise warm water pours from a metal pipe located over the cut out. Within minutes the tub is full. Leaping into the water, I feel the warm liquid caress my skin. All the muck in my hair mixes with the clear water, giving it a brown tint. Using all the soaps, oils, and ointments possible, I feel like I just went beneath a cleansing lake and came out pure. After my bath, I dry myself with a soft velvet towel and slip into the robe provided. Leaving my dirty clothes in the bath house, I spot Father John waiting for me at a table reading one of the many books available on the dozen shelves around us. Smiling, he takes me to the dining room. Laid out before me are several different cheeses, meats, and breads. Filling my plate, I scarf down the food without any hesitation and drink all the water in my goblet.

I was famished.

Then after singing a few songs, participating in a prayer, and enjoying a casual chat with Father John which I didn't even know was possible, I find myself cozy in a spare bed. It is just as nice as my bed at my father's house and looks very similar as well. The room is only different because of the several decorations consisting of crosses and statues of Jesus, but otherwise it's like sleeping at my father's place. Except, I actually feel safe and welcomed here.

* * *

Waking from a nightmare, I catch my breath. I dreamt The Beast devoured the church with darkness. Sweating, I sigh.

Mumbling proceeds from the library.

I don't think I'm dreaming. I pinch myself. *Definitely not.*

Sliding out of bed, I creep outside my room. Entering one of many paths that are evenly spread from one end of the library to the other as rays of sunlight, I crawl on my hands and feet behind a shelf of dusty, antiquated books. A single flickering oil lamp in the hand of Father John illuminates his face. Four other men I recognize as elders of the church stand in a circle around him, their faces being riddled with dancing shadows. Their coal black eyes give no impression of joy. Fidgeting, the elderly men stare at Father John without breaking their gazes even once, like they're in some sort of trance. Father John speaks in a hushed tone and keeps a still face. His eyes look no different than the four in the circle with him. They are lifeless and seem to glisten with clouds of tears ready to pour down his sunken cheeks.

"They have called our decision to honor King Oscar as treason against their law and as blasphemy towards God. They also call us cowards for siding with King Oscar and say we fear him more than The Beast itself. There is no doubt in my mind they will be here any moment," Father John says solemnly, not looking up from the ground.

"They cannot possibly bring calamity to the church. This is a holy place," protests one of the four elders.

"To them it is merely a building. To them the church is merely a structure. They have no reason not to

126

destroy it. Their logic overpowers their feeble beliefs," Father John replies.

Wiping my sweaty palms against the floor, I feel the moisture in my mouth dry like a desert.

Who is coming?

Distant shouts echo through the library, and the sound of a door rattling is also heard.

Looking up at his fellow elders, Father John says, "Let us take communion."

I hadn't noticed that in his other hand, Father John had a bottle of wine and a half loaf of bread. Tearing chunks from the bread after passing his lamp to the elder on his right, Father John hands each one of them a piece. They all eat at once. A door snaps, letting out a shout that echoes throughout the room. The elders don't flinch. I hear the screaming mob break through the sanctuary.

Passing around the bottle of wine, the elders and Father John all take a swig and say amen. The elders walk in a line out towards the sanctuary with their heads low and hands crossed at their legs. However, Father John stays behind and sits at a chair with the bottle of wine in hand. The oil lamp is no longer lit and sits by his feet. Running over to Father John, I shake him frantically.

"We must go, Father. We must go!" I scream, pulling at his arm. I can hear the shrieks of death out in the sanctuary. Four of them to be precise.

Staring at the hallway that leads to the sanctuary, he replies, "No child, they will not stop till their blood thirst is quenched. They are finished with me and have no room in their cold hearts for God's message." Taking another swig from his bottle, he continues, "I shall drink the bitter cup of death and taste my own blood. I shall drink the same cup as my savior did, except he was able to save mankind and I was only able to spare for a short time a broken kingdom."

Tipping back the bottle, Father John swallows another large gulp of wine before a horde of men come sprinting down the hallway. With knives, machetes, swords, and daggers, they tackle him, breaking his chair and spearing him like a fish. Weeping, I walk towards my room, unable to look at Father John as he takes his final breath in the hands of monsters. In the hands of blood-thirsty barbarians. I can hear their grunting and, screaming and the moans of Father John as they gut his body like a stag after the hunt.

Glass shatters; I can smell the pungent wine spill all over the floor.

The church bells overhead strike twelve.

Chapter 21

All day, from morning to night, the mob resides inside the church ripping apart books, consuming all the food, and making merry by the table of wine they set up in the library over Father John's blood-soaked body. I only come out of the spare room once in hope to find cheese to satisfy my hunger. Scurrying through the library as quickly as possible, I notice that every book is shredded, and every ornament is shattered. Partially eaten food is smashed into the floor, and puddles of strong drink cover the entire room, whether it be a bookshelf or the floor. Yet drunk and merry everyone laughs, joining in knife throwing competitions as if nothing had just happened. That is why I keep to myself, away from the mad crowd in the library. A few times as I was in my room, a few stupors stumbled in cursing and laughing, but otherwise I'm mostly left alone. Left to cry. Left to mourn. Left to sleep.

Waking, I hear no giddy chatter, no deep chuckling, or angry grunting from two sots that are wrestling over the last piece of cheese or last gulp of wine. Slipping out of bed and still wearing the robe provided for me by Father John, I drowsily walk out into the library. Many lay passed out on the floor or across chairs, and some are stacked on top of each other in an unsorted manner causing the couch they lie on to bow. Creeping slowly across the library so not to arouse anyone, I come by the bath house door. Opening the door just enough for me to slip inside, I notice a man and a woman naked together in the tub. Both asleep, the woman's head lies on the back of the man's shoulder as his head rests on her breasts. Long black hair tucked behind her back and pinned against the end of the tub reaches the woman's buttocks. It is the woman with beautiful black hair sleeping with Austin Puntions. Wrapped around her waist, both of Austin's mighty arms meet together pressed against the side of her thigh where a large splotch of dark blood pools beneath her skin. Her thigh and waist are discolored a deep crimson color, and her breasts are laced with protruding red scratch marks that look like they belong to a fox.

Swallowing the lump hanging in my throat, I scope the bath house for my clothing. Thrown in the corner to my right are my dirty rags. Tip-toeing over, I sweep them up into my arms. Gently closing the bath house door, I go out into the sanctuary. No one can be found. Changing there, I leave the wool robe that kept me warm for so long on one of the benches closest to me. The church doors hang open, and only a sliver of light can be seen over the horizon. Walking outside, I feel a nip in the brisk morning air unusual for such a time in the year. Making my way towards The Square, I notice unusual decorations on townhouse walls and by the streets. There are red eyes, disfigured hands, and crude wooden statues to resemble a particular snake, I believe a king cobra. One house even had the words "May not my soul be damned today" written with black ink over its door. Beyond the cult like figures disgracing the kingdom, I sense a dark presence all around me, like a cloud hanging over my head. Disturbed, I divert my eyes away from the buildings around me and towards The Square within my sights. Freezing at about twenty paces from city-square, I notice dozens of guards with bows in hand standing on The Square. Hundreds more pace up and down city-square.

Sneaking into a nearby alley way, I find a stack of stones at the end of it reaching the roof of the townhouse to its right. Climbing my way onto the flat stone roof, I crawl on my belly behind the chimney to protect myself from the sight of the guards. Huddling behind the rough stone chimney, I peer around the corner with one eye. A whole army regiment forms a wall blocking all the passageways into the other side of the city. They are not simple guards, either; most of them wear iron armor and stand with their backs straight and heads high. They are actual soldiers bred for war. Scuttling back towards the stone pile, I jump down. There is no possible way I can get across without being seen. Heaving a sigh, I slump over and dawdle back towards the church. I'm not ready to face my father. Even if I was, I fear I may get killed by the soldiers as a rebel.

When I am almost at the church, I hear a cackle. A shriek almost. Not a shriek of terror, but of sadistic joy. To my left, plenty of smoke rises towards the sky. It doesn't rise from a chimney either, but rather from a pitted lane. My spirit trembles, but my legs move forward anyway. Scattered across the lane are many black feathers and drops of blood. The townhouses around me seem to be vacant as they both seem to crumble and cave in on themselves. Loosely placed, the cobblestones making up the lane wobble and rock as I step on them. Shivering, I try to keep my teeth from chattering. The unseen darkness I sensed earlier now seems to grow stronger as I proceed farther. Shadows watch over me as the morning sun breaks over the horizon. It's not a beautiful pink and orange glow, but rather a sickly pale yellow. Deeper into the lane I go. Crawling up my arm, my skin becomes clammy as the aura of darkness around me swallows me whole. The morning light disappears behind a towering stone building that seems to have been left there to rot for years. As sickly as the morning light was, its absence raises my fears. Utter darkness consumes me.

A fire made from dry brush and sun baked logs crackles at the end of the lane. It is my only source of light. Stalking closer, I scan the end of the lane with suspicion. I fail to swallow my saliva because there is nothing to swallow. My mouth is as dry as it can get. Blowing on my hair, a breeze sends a chill down my back. Turning around, I back closer to the fire. Its warmth is inviting. A breeze chills my back again. Spinning around, I see the fire reach for the heavens, but the smoke is sable. Darker than a moonless sky. Shivering, my spine registers another breeze sensation. Sucking in my breath, I turn around again. Frozen in place, I breathe heavily. A cackle echoes off the walls. Swooping down at my face, a crow screeches and, in a fury of feathers, vanishes into the air. I sweat, hearing my heart pound against my chest like a hammer. Swooping down at me, another crow nearly rips my nose off. A figure of darkness appears from the sky, a cloaked devil that snatches the bird up in its hands with a shrill laugh.

It cannot be a devil

Unveiling its cloak with the crow still in hand, the devil turns out to be a woman. A woman that age did not treat kindly. Deep crevices burrow into her cheeks and her eyes are embedded deeper into her skull. Her hair, static, is a disgusting gray that parts down the center. Her thin lips and pointy chin draw attention to her four-tooth smile. Strangely, it is her canine teeth that remain as they seem to be filed down to sharp points. She is like a wingless bat, or just simply a hag. Digging her hawk like talons into the bird's chest, she crushes the bird's sternum then, with god-like strength, tears it open. Guffawing hysterically, she lets the blood run down into the fire, then without a word she throws the bird into the hot ashes beneath the burning logs. Turning blacker, the smoke rises higher with a strong odor belonging to only death.

I try to collect my disarrayed thoughts. I am befuddled by my fear. I wish I could run, but I don't. I wish I could flee, but I can't. With bloodstained hands, the witch approaches me and digs her nails into the back of my shoulder blades. Her breath smells bitter, like she lives off raw birds.

132

"What do you want?" she asks with a dry raspy voice.

I remain silent. My voice was scared away a while ago.

Looking behind her, she returns her beady eyes on me and smiles, saying, "The Beast is to come. The crows know. They predict the future. Do you want to know? Do you want to know what is to come?"

I shake my head, but not with confidence. Laughing, she pulls me closer to the fire; she grapples my wrist. Taking out a blade from the inside of her cloak, she slices open my hand. Wincing, I try to pull it back, but her strength is far greater than mine. Holding my hand over the fire, she lets my blood mingle with the blood of the burning crow. Screams echo inside my head and chanting rings in my ears. Imploding, my focus turns inward, and my worst fantasies become reality as I find myself in another world void of light.

Images, many images, fly by my mind. Images of fire, smoke, war, and of an ominous figure I cannot describe but only know to be The Beast. It lives in everything I see, but its physical form seems to be cloaked behind a veil of mortality. Only the immortal can fully understand its power, but any can witness its destruction. Internal destruction. Destruction of more than a kingdom, but also the spirits of those susceptible to its deception. Then like a celestial force pulled me back into reality, I focus on the fire and hear the cackles of the witch who still holds my wrist.

Stumbling backwards, I pull my bleeding hand close to my chest that rises and falls rapidly. Frantically searching the alley way for the witch, I can't spot her.

Run.

Sprinting, I try to escape. I try to escape the witch, but much more I try to escape the images in my head. But I can't.

Chapter 22

Dusk settles over the land. Peering over the crest of the horizon, stars glisten. I huddle in a corner hugging my knees. I am in the room that I slept in last night. All the townspeople are out doing whatever it is they desire to do. I peeked outside not too long ago, just before the sun fell beneath the earth, to see if anyone was coming back, but I saw no one. Rocking back and forth, I count the seconds that go by. The vision given to me by the witch haunts my thoughts. The screams of terror. The visages of the dead. The hot embers of hell. They have branded my mind.

I rock back and forth hoping that somehow I can rock away my troubles. That in some way they may fly away and never return. Passing minutes promise me that the images in my head will never go away. Rather they will become more and more vivid as the days go on. Looming over me, a heavy darkness, like a spiritual presence, keeps me company. Not company I have invited, but rather company that has invaded my spirit.

I continue to rock back and forth. Night closes in on the kingdom. A light rain begins to fall as the raindrops dance on the rooftops. It has been days since rain has fallen over the city, and now it has come. Farmers undoubtedly are happy at the present moment. Allowing myself to relax, I let go of my knees. Closing my eyes, I focus on the sound of the rain hitting the church's roof. Breathing in and out, I try to let the images drain from my memories. My head hurts. My stomach churns. I can feel the bruises and aches all over my body. I do not feel well. The more I try to relax, the more pain I seem to feel. Clenching my muscles, the pain dulls, but the images rage on.

Tears wet my cheeks. I wish I could undo what I have seen. I wish I could undo it all. I wish I could go back in time before our kingdom became so divided. Before The Beast. Before Jonah.

* * *

At some point, I must have rocked myself to sleep because I woke up with a crick in my neck from leaning against the wall. Thunder roars in the heavens. Steady sheets of rain collide with the roof. Yet there seems to be another noise. The noise of nervous chatter. The sound of men groaning. Walking out into the library, I come across several men, women, and children. Blood pools across the floor. Most the men are bleeding out from every part of their bodies. The women attend to them as the children stand around, not knowing what to do. The entire area became a makeshift medical office overnight.

There are bandages, natural remedies, and buckets of water all over the place. Walking aimlessly into the center of the chaos, I notice rough looking men guarding the entrance to the library with military grade spears. I'm surprised I wasn't woken up until just now. Standing by the bookshelf closest to me is a boy no older than ten wearing nothing besides his undergarments. Approaching the skittish child who twiddles his thumbs, I go on my knees. He stares at me with blank eyes. He shakes like the wind is bustling around his body. Grabbing his arms, I feel that they are cold to the touch.

"What is going on?" I ask.

Opening his mouth, he tries to answer me, but nothing comes out. I repeat the question. Stammering, he glances back and forth. I grab his hands. Focusing, he looks at me.

136

"What is happening?"

"They came," he whispers.

"Who?"

"Weasels."

As he says that, a bloody man screaming at the top of his lungs is being dragged into the library. Drenched like a fish, the man is missing an entire arm.

There is no way he can live losing that much blood, I think.

Letting him lie in the middle of the floor, one of the men on guard duty goes running around the church in search of a doctor. In less than a minute, the guard is tugging a weary old man down the main corridor towards the library. A man I know as Doctor Commons, but no longer does he look as wise as he did. Rather he appears to have aged by twenty years in the past couple days. Sagging below his eyes, his skin is blotchy. It melts off his bones like snow. Emptier than the last time I saw him, he slides his feet like they're boulders. He pays no attention to the moans, the cries, and the groans of pain like he would have weeks ago. Instead, he fixes his eyes on the feet of the guard dragging him towards the one-armed man. Falling onto his knees, Dr. Commons unravels the bandage he has in his right hand. He has a small flask in in his left hand that he douses the bandage with.

Weaving in between frantic women, buckets of water, and wounded men, I stand by Doctor Commons.

"Doc," I say. He doesn't even flinch. He keeps attending to the one-armed man who is blatantly dead. His crying has ceased, and his chest is no longer moving. Oblivious, Doctor Commons continues to wrap the stub on the dead man.

"Doctor Commons," I say louder.

Raising his ears, he stops what he is doing. Looking up at me slowly, he gives no sign of recognition.

"What?" he croaks.

"What are you doing here?"

"Don't badger me. I already know that answer," he replies, gazing down at my bare feet. He has reached the epitome of despair. Clinging onto the little sanity he has left, he burned any sense of individuality he had.

"Doc, it's me. It's Thomas."

Ignoring me, Doctor Commons begins to mumble, "I am here as a slave. A slave to attend to dying men, as I shall be if I disobey."

My name, my existence, doesn't draw any life from his spirit. Downcast and trodden over, he acts like his life has been stolen from him. Like he forgot who he was or what his purpose is. Or even worse, he found out that now he is purposeless.

"Doc, stop this," I whisper, kneeling by his side and touching his arm. It is like touching wet, tattered, leather.

Pulling back his arm, he hides his face from me.

"Please, sir. Do not strike me. Not while I attend to this ailed man."

"I am not going to strike you. Doc, it is me."

Crying, Doctor Commons pleads for me to leave him. He begs me to stop hurting him, but I have already let go of him.

"Leave him alone, boy," growls one of the spearmen, throwing me over his shoulder.

Weeping still, Doctor Commons huddles in a ball. Concealing himself from the world around him, he lets out his pain. Pain that I have never witnessed before. Pain I could never imagine. Bitter tears burn his eyes.

The clock strikes twelve.

Chapter 23

A small militia, no bigger than three hundred men, caught many rebels off guard. No one was expecting a raid at night. Quickly, the militia tore through the northwest section of the kingdom, eliminating the unexpecting rebels rather quickly. The militia was going to continue farther into the west side of the kingdom because they suffered very few casualties; however, Austin gathered together a small band of men to face the militia. When the two forces met, there was plenty of bloodshed. Then, like The Beast itself sided with the rebels, the militia fled out of pure fear like they had all seen a ghost, leading to a victory for the rebels. This is all according to a report brought to the church by a scraggly messenger boy about my age wearing a weird, feathery hat. He spoke like a king with great charisma and expressive hand gestures, telling the news like some sort of legendary war tale. Most of what he said was obvious propaganda, but all the townspeople loved it as they whooped and cheered. Even the wounded let out small cheers. The only one I saw remaining quiet besides myself was Doctor Commons. Nothing in the world could make him smile again.

"No way those weasels will be back anytime soon!" the messenger boy proclaims.

"When will Austin be back so we can bring him honor?" asks a pudgy fellow with an eye patch.

"As soon as he can," replies the messenger.

"Mighty fine man. Ought to be king." The crowd agrees with a loud applause.

How can he be any better than Oscar?

"Austin the Great will rise to the throne one day!" shouts the messenger, jumping onto an upside down bucket and raising his burnt torch in the air with his hand over his eyes like the sun is beating down upon him.

"I commit myself to Austin the Great!" hollers the pudgy fellow with an eye patch.

"As do I!" shouts a skinnier fellow and another and another until everyone joins in chanting Austin the Great.

The messenger does a jig on the bucket while raising his hand at one side of the crowd so that they get louder than to the other. He also puts his hand to his ear and says, "I can't hear you." It's a rally. A rally after a victorious battle. Everyone is having a great time besides me. Rather, I feel sick to my stomach. Heading back to my room, I close my ears blocking out the chanting. I got a terrible headache as well. Going back to bed, I try to fall asleep. To take a nap. To, in a way, sleep away my troubles.

* * *

Tired, I sleep for hours upon hours until I can sleep no longer. Loud chatter proceeds from the library. There is never a dull moment at the church. Someone is either in great pain, great elation, or greatly drunk. Leaving my room, I spot Austin instantly. Creating a pedestal out of books, he stands before everyone with a simple crown upon his head. In the center of the iron crown is a cross, but on his bare body scarred from war is a crimson eye created with war paint. A large, splotchy scar also marks the left side of his face, making it look like it's peeling off. Everyone is talking among themselves about how brave Austin is or about his heroic feats in the last battle, and the women can be heard talking about his handsome figure. The only ones not talking about Austin are those recovering from wounds. Most of them just groan. Some seem to be angling their heads to get a glimpse of "Austin the Great."

"Attention!" Austin proclaims, raising a fist in the air. Going silent, everyone listens with anticipation. "Yesterday was the beginning of war. King Oscar may be too cowardly to declare official war, but according to my standards, any invasion is an act of war. They have started this dispute, but we will be the ones to settle it. Today we devise a plan to bring the war to them." Clapping, his audience agrees. He continues, "Listen up! The men not wounded will be expected to fight in this war, or at least aid to the cause."

"Anyone who doesn't will be killed," interjects the pudgy fellow with an eye patch.

"Indeed," Austin replies, "either you go to a designated post or you help build the catapults."

"Catapults?" Doctor Commons asks in a shrill voice.

Shocked, I stare at Doctor Commons with my mouth hanging open. Never once did he raise his voice until now as he kneels by a man with a disfigured face. It is like someone took a club to it and mixed the positions of where his mouth, nose, and eyes are supposed to be.

"Yes, catapults so we can destroy The Manor from a distance and bring hell down upon those wealthy bastards."

Whooping, the crowd punches the air or slaps each other's backs.

"That is foolish. You are now becoming the monster," Doctor Commons says, rising to his feeble feet. Knocking together, his legs curve inward.

What has possessed Doctor Commons?

Scowling, Austin gets down from his pedestal and approaches Doctor Common so that he is nose to nose with him.

"I am not a monster. Now kiss my feet and apologize, scum. Or I'll feed you to the crows."

Shaking, Doctor Commons' back is turned towards me. He fiddles around. Wobbling, it looks like his legs are about to buckle. It's like he's internally fighting himself. Austin waits straight-faced. If Doctor Commons submits, he admits defeat.

Looking down at Austin's feet, he drools on them, which I think was meant to be a spit, and says, "Dying is better than being a slave to a stone hearted monster."

Cursing, Austin socks Doctor Commons across the face, knocking him over. Teeth fly and blood spurts from his mouth as Doctor Commons hits the ground, lying prostrate on the floor.

"No!" I shriek, ramming my body against Austin. He barely budges. Swinging an elbow at my face, he nails me. Falling over, I get right back up and shove him again. Grabbing me by my throat, he punches me in the face repeatedly till all I can see is red and blue.

Throwing me onto the ground, he bellows, "Brand the Doctor!"

I hear someone being dragged across the floor groaning, but I can't see a thing besides red and blue. I hear a crackling fire, but all I can feel is my face swelling. I can hear Doctor Commons grunting as the sound of men beating him silences the room, but all I can taste is bitter blood. Waiting in agony to hear more, I bite my tongue so I don't curse over the pain I feel.

"Brand him," I hear Austin say. Blood-curdling cries rip apart my ears. Screaming like he is dying, Doctor Commons gives me an ear-splitting headache. Crying, I beg for them to stop. To stop whatever it is their doing, but they don't. It continues for what seems like ages. I weep. It hurts to cry, but there is nothing else I can do. Until a cackle breaks the screams.

"Now let the fool sleep, then tomorrow we feed him to The Beast," says Austin. Moans escape Doctor Commons' lips, yet all I can see is red and blue.

*   *   *

Staggering, Doctor Commons, in shackles, submits to the men with spears. Shackled as well, I watch. I pull at the chains around my wrists, but I'm held against a post that is impossible for a little rat like me to pull apart. I am no Samson. They take Doctor Commons to the main corridor.

"What are you doing?" I ask. Tears stain my cheeks. All morning since nightfall they have been needling me with cruel jokes, mocking my black and blue eye or calling Doctor Commons names.

They would say, "Would he be better a Christmas ornament? A dangling black and red ornament? Maybe you'd like to see him be chopped up limb by limb. Maybe—"

Then I'd start screaming till they'd slap me, reinvigorating the pain in my swollen face. I can see now, but I can't decide whether or not I'm glad I can. Austin leads a couple spear-men. Stopping at the hallway door, he raises his hand. Turning around, he looks at me.

"You want to watch?" he asks with a twisted smile. I shake my head. He says, "Don't be silly. Somebody bring this boy along."

Another man with a spear unshackles me from the post. Jerking me along, he doesn't let me stay back. Giving up, I follow. Chuckling, Austin continues forward as do the men with spears. In shambles, the sanctuary is unrecognizable. Benches are flipped upside down, right side up, or smashed into splinters. Every stained-glass window is shattered, and every religious ornament is on the floor. My heart drops all the way down to my stomach.

Never once this morning could I see Doctor Commons' face. I picture tears welling up in his eyes. I picture him falling apart inside. I picture him dead. Shaking my head, I try to shake away the image of him

143

dangling from the gallows. Getting closer to city-square, I question Austin's intentions.

He doesn't intend to face a wall of soldiers, alone does he?

Taking a sharp right, we march down a crummy alley. Chills run up my spine and a cold sweat breaks out all over my body. The witch.

"What are you doing?" I ask. Straining my neck, I lean as far forward as I can in hopes to get a glimpse of Austin's expression.

"Something wrong?" he asks in reply, not bothering to look over his shoulder at me.

"You're a damn fool!" I cry.

Coming to a halt, Austin holds up the spearmen. Spinning around on the heels of his feet, he approaches me. Not fast, but slowly like each step means something to him. Just like my father. Expressionless, he bends over so he is at my eye level. Ice water chills my veins; I freeze. Petrified, I glance down at his hand hidden beneath his cloak. Not breaking his stare, he focuses on my eyes. Drawing his dagger, he leans closer. I try to back up, but my spearman presses his hand against the back of my neck. Raspy, I breathe in spurts of thick air. Grabbing the nape of my neck, Austin pulls me closer.

Still staring he whispers, "Do you know what my father told my little brother when he was just a boy?"

I shake my head.

"He used to say, 'Silence is golden,' whenever he wagged his tongue at him. Then one day, after my brother raised his voice at father, he went berserk and took my mother's kitchen knife and cut my brother's tongue off!" Trying to pry my mouth open with his blade, he screams, "Open that damn mouth!" Tearing open my mouth, Austin grabs hold of my tongue, squeezing it tighter than a python and nearly ripping it off. Raising his dagger, he swings down, but it clashes with an iron chain. Standing behind Austin is Doctor Commons holding his shackles in the way of the blade. Time stops for only a second as I

144

take in Doctor Commons' face. Branded on his forehead is a cruel eye. The eye of The Beast. Down his cheeks streak burn wounds like claws. Sewed shut, his mouth is unable to be opened. He looks like a puppet. A demented puppet made to be an offering for The Beast.

"Go to hell you bastard!" bellows Austin, swinging the handle of his blade around, clobbering Doctor Commons in the cheek. I grind my teeth. I wish I could beat them all up, light them all on fire and watch, but I can't. Grunting, Doctor Commons falls onto his knees. His face grows red from holding in his wails. Kicking him in the gut, Austin curses him again, sliding his blade back into his cloak.

"Let us go, Crow Mother does not like waiting," Austin growls.

Dragging Doctor Commons, the spearmen hurry to keep up with Austin. I move my feet in step with my spearman. The morning sun hides behind the giant stone building at the end of the alley. Again, a fire is lit where it was the last time I came here. Crow Mother stands by the fire with a massive crow on her shoulder. Her black, wiry, hair covers her shoulders. Stepping closer to Doctor Commons, she examines his face with her four-tooth grin. Nodding her head, a gleam strikes her eye.

"My, a fine specimen. I sense such intellect," she says.

"Of course, Mother," Austin replies humbly with a slight bow.

"He has a defiant spirit, however. He believes The Beast is a foe, not an ally. Ignorant. The real beasts are the tyrants in The Manor."

"Yes, Mother. Will he do?"

"Of course. The Beast craves such a kind as this."

"Then perform the ritual, Mother."

"Of course."

Kicking out Doctor Commons' legs, Austin makes him kneel. But Doctor Commons cannot stay still. He tries to run. He tries to flee frantically, but digging her claws into his shoulder, the Crow Mother clutches him tightly. Shaking like an earthquake is rampaging through his frail body, Doctor Commons grunts for help. I try to move but am immediately swatted across the head with the butt of a spear. Gouging out his eyes with the same blade she cut me with, Crow Mother throws Doctor Commons onto the cobblestone street. Pounding the ground with his fists, he bleeds out on the cobblestone. An ocean of murky blood spills into the cracks between the stones running down my direction. Throwing herself on top of him, Crow Mother carves a cross into his bare back. Shaking his head and jolting his body, he tries to escape, but she overpowers him. The crow that used to be on her shoulder squawks overhead, and a flock of crows gather together in the sky like a black storm cloud. Taking a chunk of his flesh, Crow Mother throws it into the fire, and immediately the flock of demon birds swarm his body. They squawk, they bicker, they claw at the expense of Doctor Commons' life. Tears stream down my face. My tears mingle with the blood of Doctor Commons. Innocent blood. The only innocent blood remaining besides Jonah's. Gone.

Chapter 24

A prisoner. I suppose that's what I am. Not only physically, but emotionally. Running through my mind as I sleep, or attempt to sleep, are all the memories of Doctor Commons. Austin was nice enough to allow me to sleep on the bed again, but I fear that sort of generosity will not last. Though it doesn't really matter. I hardly want to live as is. Merely sleeping on the floor would mean little to me. Death never seemed so inviting. Yet there still seems to be a voice inside me telling me not to give up. Maybe a faint sense of optimism. A stroke of hope. Whatever it may be, it gets quieter every day. Midnight strikes. I toss and I turn as I hear Doctor Commons hack up blood after a crow tore apart the string bounding his mouth shut. I see his eyes being torn from his skull as the Crow Mother feasts off his fear. Tears stain my pillow as they stained my cheeks the day before.

Then when my painful nightmare ends, I spot Jonah. He crouches somewhere hiding from all the chaos. I can't say where. I can only say that in my dream, I see him sobbing over the madness he feels responsible for. Though I personally cannot blame him for any of it. I can only blame the people who have run from common sense and found refuge beneath the cover of insanity. Liberty seems to be absent from the picture now as a larger threat lies at hand — internal destruction.

"Get up, wretch," says a spearman swinging my door open.

Throwing the blanket over my face, I refuse to get up. Tired from lack of sleep, I hope the spearman will leave me alone, but he doesn't.

Grabbing the back of my tunic, he throws me onto the floor. My blanket gets caught between my legs, falling on top of me. Ramming the butt of his spear into my side, he yells, "Get up!"

Crawling out from beneath the blanket, I rise to my feet. My spearman, a tall person with a lean figure and ratty leather armor stolen from a dead weasel, tugs me out the room.

"You're helping with the catapults," he says, pushing me along out to the sanctuary.

It's not too early. The sun is over the city and some people are out on the streets. Everyone, even children and women, have weapons. One child no older than ten had a double-edged sword in hand as he followed his mother carrying a woven basket which I could only assume had a dagger at the bottom of it as a sharp point stuck out from it.

Marching deeper into the west side, I find myself on streets I never explored before, but I can now tell why so many people hate King Oscar. Lying on blankets and huddling together, families too poor to afford homes cough and wheeze as they try to sleep. People skinnier than me live in the same type of alleyways the witch inhabits. The children play with stones, throwing them at each other or stacking them up into towers, since they can't afford real toys. The parents just try to survive by scrounging up whatever food they have available. Townhouses this deep into the west side of the kingdom can barely fit four people in them comfortably, they are that small. Also, thousands of rats scurry about claiming every crumb they can for themselves. They steal from those who are starving. Some people have raided homes making them their own as many houses have broken windows or doors without hinges and dozens of people crammed inside them guarding their doors with homemade traps like speared floors or doors with arrows protruding out from them so that unwanted guests will suffer if those inside slam the door in the intruder's face.

Deeper into the west side we go till we reach a small clearing like a miniature city-square just for the west side. A base for an enormous catapult has been already started. Many of the rebels slave away, whether it be out of will or reluctance. Some look like former soldiers who now serve as war prisoners. Many rebels that take themselves too seriously circle the area making sure no workers try to leave without consent. Those working on the catapults hammer together planks of wood while others carry supplies.

"Now, you listen to Troy," my spearman says.

"Who is that?" I ask.

"That one," he replies, pointing at an older gentleman sitting in a wooden chair supervising the entire operation.

Troy occasionally shouts at someone to work harder or to pick up something, but otherwise seems to keep to himself. Approaching him, I find myself having flashbacks.

Doctor Commons?

Wearing large spectacles which are slightly cracked, Troy looks almost identical to Doctor Commons before he was Austin's prisoner, and before he was killed

Rubbing my face, I try to hide the forming tears at the corners of my eyes. Angling his head my direction, Troy raises his eyebrows and asks, "Yes?"

He would be a twin to Doctor Commons if it wasn't for his eyes. Dark. Very dark. They seem to be sucking in any light around them and destroying it.

"I was told to ask you what I should do," I say timidly.

Sighing, he looks around the clearing till his eyes fall upon an area with a pile of boulders.

"You have any experience with catapults?" he asks.

"No, sir."

"Aye, as I expected. So, I want you to shimmy those rocks over there behind the two forming catapults. Ain't any reason why they shouldn't be ready as soon as possible."

"What good does that do?"

Looking at me puzzled, he replies, "Can't have the boulders way over there when we engage these apparatuses. They must be in a position of use."

"Why now?"

"Ain't gonna trust you with construction. Now skedaddle, boy. Do as you're told." Waving his hand, he shoos me away.

Reluctantly, I move over to the pile of rocks. Clambering on top of the stack of boulders, I try to lift the top one which is four times the size of my head. Gritting my teeth and pulling with all my might, I can only lift the rock a few inches off the stack. Dropping it back down again, I catch my breath.

"Better be able to do more than that, boy," Troy scoffs from his chair. Someone must have gotten him a glass of wine because he now sips on some sort of vermilion liquid.

Lazy ass, I think to myself.

Putting my back against the top rock, I push with my legs so I can roll it down the pile. Lifting out of its divot, it begins to tumble down the rocks, then it strikes another rock which kicks out as well, and soon the entire side begins sliding onto the street. Falling, I crack my elbow against another stone which flips me sideways in the air. Tumbling onto the cobblestone clearing, I bite my tongue. Gritting my teeth, I punch the ground.

I cannot scream, I think to myself even though that is all I want to do. Not only because of my fall, but for Doctor Commons, because Austin is a monster, and because I want things to go back to how they use to be. Peaceful.

"Dammit, boy," Troy says, getting out of his seat. I rest on my knees now holding my right elbow.

Another black and blue mark, I think to myself. I have so many over my body. It is a wonder how I can still get around.

"Get up," Troy says, grabbing the back side of my tunic. Raising me to my feet, he examines me with his sable eyes. "You are skinnier than a starved rabbit. Ain't an inch of meat on your sorry hide." Pinching my arm, he shakes his head in disapproval. "I ain't got no room for useless scrubs like you." looking at my spearman, he motions him over. "Tell Austin to take this one back. I don't want this pathetic vermin." Mumbling curses, Troy walks back to his chair to continue sipping on his wine.

"Come with me, boy," my spearman says, obviously irritated. He probably thinks he has wasted his time with me. Marching quietly back to the church, I cannot help but feel angry. A runt. That is what I am. A runt. I couldn't save Doctor Commons. I couldn't stand up to my father whenever he beat me over Mother's death, whether he was drunk or sober. Growing up, I was always the one running away from the bullies. I would always lose my fights. I am just a failure. I am useless.

Austin's temper was boiling hot when he heard Troy found me "inadequate" according to my spearman who told the whole story of me ruining the pile of rocks. Slapping me, Austin shoves me onto the floor. Shackling me again, he chains me to the post I was on yesterday. Handing a whip to my spearman, he says, "Flog this bastard."

Nodding, the spearman takes the leather whip with shards of glass in it and cracks it against my back. Gagged, I can't scream, but only cry.

Second strike.

Third strike.

Fourth strike.

I sob. Snot coats my lips, and tears lather my cheeks. Balling my hands up into fists, I slide onto my knees.

Fifth strike.

151

Sixth strike.

Seventh strike.

Weeping, I feel the skin on my back peel away. My tunic is torn into ribbons.

Eighth strike.

Ninth strike.

Tenth strike.

My back feels so raw. I feel paralyzed. I feel like I am going to die.

Eleventh strike.

Twelfth strike.

Thirteenth strike.

Digging my nails into my palms, I lose feeling in my legs.

Fourteenth strike.

Fifteenth strike.

I hear Austin say something. I feel something. I think shackles coming off, but it is too hard to tell. Lights. Time. Strikes twelve. Darkness.

Chapter 25

Jonah. Apparently, it was him who released me. He is the reason I now lie on my stomach in the room I claimed as mine in the church. He came back yesterday afternoon to speak with Austin. For what purpose? That I have yet to figure out. Not like I am in any position to get up and ask him. Still in great pain, I stay as still as I can. Any movement I make I can feel the remaining glass in my back cut farther into my skin. Jonah apparently took out most the glass shards he could, but he missed a few. This is according to my spearman who needs to check on me every hour. So, I do not know how much I can believe him. I would ask him to remove the remaining glass if I would actually expect him to do so.

If Jonah is back, then maybe that means he will nullify Austin's intensity. But I doubt it. After watching Austin yesterday, I really doubt anything will keep him from his sole purpose of taking over this kingdom. Wincing, I feel a surge of pain shoot up my back. According to my spearman, some of my spine is sticking out of my back and that is why I have chills. That I hope is a lie. No way fifteen strikes against the back can do all that. Unless I miscounted. Impossible.

"How are you?" The voice isn't deep like my spearman's voice; it's squeakier. Opening my eyes, I see the stomach belonging to a pudgy fellow in a simple black robe. Jonah.

"Not too well," I reply weakly.

"I suppose that would be the correct answer," he says. Standing over me, he inspects my back, then a few sharp pinches cause me to suck in air. "Sorry. I was getting rid of some of that glass. Such cruelty should never fall upon children."

"It is quite all right. It didn't hurt," I lie.

"Good to hear," he says doubtfully. I'm too easy to read.

"What are you here for?" I ask.

Rubbing his head, he sighs, "To end this foolishness."

"Foolishness?"

"This ongoing war between King Oscar and his own people. They all are supposed to come together as one body. Helping one another. Yet they bicker and fight like enemies."

"How did that fellow respond?"

"Austin? Not so well. It is far too late to convince him otherwise." Shaking his head, Jonah continues, "Enough of that. I came here to raise your spirits, not to tear them down. How may I help you?"

"Well, by freeing me from this hell hole," I mutter.

"I doubt I could get far with that. Especially in your condition."

"That is a shame. That is all I want."

"I suppose I shall stay here with you then until you have any further commands, my liege," he jokes. Getting a chair, he leaves and comes back to sit down beside me.

It just struck me that I never really got to know Jonah. Most of the time he was on top of The Square giving some sort prophecy. I never really had conversation with him. Now it seems he is the only one I will be able to make conversation with since Doctor Commons passed. I bite my bottom lip. Don't think of him. Hold it back.

"What is your name?" Jonah asks.

"Thomas," I reply.

"Nice name."

"I guess so."

"I suppose you grew up here."

"Yes." I wince from a rush of pain that surges to my head, but it quickly passes back into its continual throbbing state.

"Are you all right?" Jonah asks, getting up as quickly as possible.

I manage to nod awkwardly on my pillow, replying, "I'm fine."

Sitting back down, he says, "I can remember my father being whipped. As a young child I would watch many prisoners be beaten, and I would laugh with a twisted pleasure inside me. Innocence I suppose blinded me from the reality of torture until the veil was lifted. My father was dragged out of our house, tied to the stake, and flogged till it seemed he had no more blood to spill."

Sniffling, Jonah dabs his eyes with a cloth stored inside his robe.

I ask, "For what reason was he beaten?"

Pausing, Jonah grabs his knees with his trembling hands, replying, "The governor over our territory thought my father was planning a mutiny based off rumor. Instead of approaching my father about it, the governor instead took harsh action by flogging him and publicly humiliating our family. It wasn't long after that my father committed suicide, causing an uproar in our small town. Some believed he was a traitor and others thought he was a good man. I only saw hurt and pain. I saw unresolved issues never settled, but merely hidden from sight until all the rocks were overturned exposing everyone's true beliefs."

I fall silent. Holding himself together, Jonah clears his throat and dabs his eyes again.

"Where was that?" I ask.

"Miles from here. A far distance away."

"Then how did you arrive here?"

Shoving his cloth back inside his robe, he replies, "I left home as soon as I could. I became a sailor for a short span of time until I grew weary of the sea. Then I took up

155

schooling and got myself an education. Yet it never seemed right to me to stay in one place, so I traveled around the country giving aid in whatever way I could to the places I passed by." Pausing, he takes a minute to bow his head and close his eyes, then as if God has spoken to him, he continues, "Then one night I had a dream of a city split just like the town I grew up in. The next day, I came across your kingdom. That is why I am here."

"What about The Beast? And what about you riding in here like some thieves clobbered you over the head?"

Shaking his head, he falls silent. I can tell by his eyes he is reflecting on something. A memory or maybe a thought. He's sifting through what he can recall only to come up blank. His eyes tell no lies.

"I don't recall that day. I can only remember riding here, then everything goes dark. I can't recall."

Frustrated, I groan as I strain my back from trying to readjust myself. I say, "You came here bruised and beaten. Then go on telling everyone about a monster or The Beast. You don't remember anything of that day you arrived. Under what incentive did you blurt such prophecies?"

Glazing over with dread, Jonah's eyes become glass. They stare into an abyss, an isolated world of his own making. Then horror grabs him by the throat. He whispers, "I saw him."

"The Beast?" I ask, knitting my eyebrows into a knot.

"Yes."

"Well?"

Grasping for words, he coughs then says, "Before my memory went blank. Before darkness consumed me. I saw him. I saw him lingering over your city with an army ready to let loose. I remember him saying that in forty days he will be coming. He just needed to prepare the city so that it would be ripe for the picking."

156

Chuckling, I reply, "I don't understand how you believe this nonsense—"

"Because it is real," he snaps. "I never witnessed something like it, and now the people are split. Now they plummet into moral depravity, and at any moment he will consume them. They did not prepare their hearts. They destroyed them."

A haze of fog blankets his eyes. A blurry memory clouds his brain. It doesn't matter whether it is true or not, because either way our city will fall either into the hands of a flamboyant king with no care for his people or the hands of an angry rebel who only thirsts for blood. Maybe there is a beast, but not in the sky. Rather it lives in us. Maybe we are The Beast.

"Does this beast have a physical form?" I ask.

"It does. Its natural state is an embodiment of pure evil, but it can take many forms of its choosing," Jonah says, still lost in his own world.

"Did you see his natural state?"

"I saw what I saw. And what I saw is nearly impossible to describe using our language. I feel it would take a supernatural language to describe how dark The Beast is."

"Are you sure you're OK?" I ask. Jonah is shivering. He is physically with me, but he is not actually with me.

"I am...but I fear no one else here is."

"What hope is there? What do you want the people to do?"

"Turn from their wickedness. Work with each other and serve the God and his Son who should be the face of this very chapel and this entire kingdom."

"That won't happen."

"That's what I fear," Jonah says, looking down at the floor. He heaves a sigh and rests his head against the wall. I don't understand Jonah, but I see that his heart is genuine. I wish I would have gotten to known him better. Maybe he could have been a second Doctor Commons to me.

But he can't.
I sigh, turning my head over towards the wall.

Chapter 26

Before nightfall, Jonah slathered my back with an ointment that made my body feel like a block of ice. Now it's morning again, and my back feels a lot better. Sitting beside me, Jonah reads a certain book he picked from one of the shelves out in the library. Mouthing each word, he looks like a cow chewing its cud. Resting on the floor beside my bed is the pasty ointment he used on my back. Licking my dry lips, I cough loudly.

Peering up from his book, Jonah smiles and says, "You are awake. How marvelous."

I smile half-heartedly, replying, "Yes."

Frowning, Jonah asks, "What's wrong?"

"My back aches. Can you use any more that ointment?"

"Of course."

Getting up, he lathers my back with the substance. It hurts like someone is tearing open every scab on my back as he applies it,, but afterwards I know it will feel amazing.

"There you go," he says.

I can already feel its effect take over. Sighing with relief, I close my eyes. I can feel it nestle deep into every wound, filling each one with its wonderful coolness.

"What is that ointment?" I ask.

Picking it up with a grin, he inspects it with a sparkle in his eye, replying, "I can't say it has a name. It was an ointment my mother taught me to make. You see we had no doctor in our little town except one that traveled from place to place, but he was only around once a month. So, we learned to take care of ourselves. This ointment is a blend of herbs and liquids."

"What herbs and liquids?"

Shaking his head, he replies, "Can't say. It is a secret."

Barging into my room, my spearman marches over to me and grabs my arm.

"In what condition are you to move?" he asks.

"Not a very good one," I say.

"What is the matter?" asks Jonah, rising to his feet.

"We were told to evacuate the church."

"What for?"

"Damon is preparing a small legion to come our way. We are moving forces in this area, but it is not safe here. So, we must go."

"I am in no condition to run," I protest.

"There is a wagon outside prepared to take all those who are wounded."

"Where are we headed?" asks Jonah.

"Towards the catapults."

"What—" I begin.

"Enough questions. We must hurry," my spearman interrupts me. Giving Jonah his spear, my spearman slides his hands underneath my chest and waist. Hoisting me into his arms, he carries me out of my room. The cool touch of the ointment seems to fade away as the pain in my back intensifies with every step my spearman takes. As soon as we're out in the sanctuary, my back feels like someone is clawing at my raw flesh.

"We are almost there," Jonah whispers. He must be able to see the agony on my scrunched-up face.

Outside, my spearman lays me down on the back of a wooden wagon with many other wounded people. I lie next to a man who must have taken a sword to the face because his entire left eye is just a bloody hole. His arm is disfigured so badly it looks like each part of it goes in a different direction.

"Get these people out of here," my spearman says.

"Yes, sir," says the driver. Cracking his whip, the driver gets the two horses to take off, lurching the wagon backwards. Wagons have awful suspension, so every bump jostles my whole body and sends surges of pain through me like lightning. Others around me must feel the same way because they groan and moans like their ghosts.

"When will this blasted trip be over?" cries a fellow behind me.

"As soon as we get there," grumbles the driver.

"Blasted weasels ruin everything," says the one-eyed man next to me. His breath smells rotten.

"They do indeed," agrees another fellow.

"That Damon ought to be hanged," says another.

Most children do not grow up hearing about how their father should die. Most. I, on the other hand, have had many occasions that someone threatened my father. It is a strange experience, especially for me. I can agree my father is a rather cruel man, but I feel guilty if I ever wish harm upon him. It is an unwinnable situation.

"How big of a legion plans on invading?" asks the one-eyed man. He doesn't ask any particular person, but says it in a way that is open for discussion.

"According to Austin, a large one," says someone behind me.

"Is Damon actually leading them?"

"Yes."

"I hope someone skewers his head on a pike," growls the one-eyed man.

"I doubt such a thing will happen," I say.

"Why is that?"

"He is far too skilled."

"So is Austin."

Keeping my thoughts to myself, I give up on arguing. Debating with patriots is practically impossible because no matter what they will always think their side is right.

"We are here!" shouts the driver, bringing the wagon to a halt.

My back is on fire. Jerking backwards, I roll over onto my side. Splinters dig into my ribs, and my back curses me for moving so abruptly.

"Damn this trip," I snarl.

In a haste, rebels carry the wounded off the wagon, not minding any of their infirmities, especially my own back. Jostling me around like a piece of meat, a giant rebel with scruff all over his face carries me by my back to another stone building. I am not able to inspect my surroundings; I am too busy closing my eyes and praying for my torture to end. Tossing me onto a stony floor, the man with scruff leaves me rolling across the stones, ignoring my cries of pain. A cellar. That's where I think I am. It is dark, the floor consists of small stones, and it smells of rotten eggs. Isolated. I am isolated.

I was told I wouldn't be left alone. I was told this by the man with scruff when he came down a second time. I almost believed him.

Chapter 27

Darkness. Absolute darkness. If it wasn't for the distant chimes of the church bell, I wouldn't know whether or not it was a new day. Hunger. Extreme hunger. I have not eaten more than bread in the past three days. Down in this dark cellar there is not a drop of water or a morsel of food. Forgotten. I must be forgotten. Left in this cellar to die and to waste away. Soon only my bones will remain in this musty cellar. Clawing at the barricaded door and spurts of screaming have brought me no success in getting help. While trying to walk in hope to learn how to cope with the bruises on my back, I cry. Tears swarm my face.

I will die if I just lie around, I continue to say in my muddy head. So, I continue to pace back and forth. Back and forth. Drying, my tears fade away. The pain in my back begins to dissipate, or maybe I am just getting use to feeling awful. My mind focuses on different topics as the throbbing in my back lessens.

Regretting my decisions. Reflecting on my life choices. Remembering those who have died.

Doctor Commons. The keeper. The keeper's wife. They all died innocent. They have done no wrong towards anyone. Their only fault was being too vulnerable. They were easy scapegoats. It is easier to kill someone who has no name or no support to appease those who do. I am also nameless. Worse, I am the son of the Devil, Damon. Being the son of the enemy makes me worse than a nobody. It makes me an enemy. Yet my young age keeps me safe, if a cellar is considered safe. I would better be described, I suppose, as a prisoner.

How well are the rebels fighting? I wonder. I can only imagine if the rebels are overpowered, I will be left to die. Forgotten. If the rebels succeed, I can only hope I am remembered. Unless my father searches for me. Yet why would my father search for me? I am the reason his wife died. Of course, I never met her. She sacrificed her life for mine as I entered this world, but I heard from Doctor Commons she was a wonderful lady. Damon used to be friendly when she was with him, but ever since he lost her, he has been bitter. Not only bitter, but also filled with hatred. Hatred mostly directed at me. There is no possible way he would ever search for me.

Time goes by. I lap up water with my tongue as drops drip from the stone ceiling. They fail to quench my thirst, but they give me hope of survival. Doctor Commons always warned me to never drink unknown water because I may get sick, yet without water I will surely die. So, I keep my tongue pressed against the gritty stone wall licking the dirty, grimy, water.

Sitting back down, I play with my fingers. Ignoring the soreness in my back, I play games with myself. I count how many stones I can hold in my hand at once or how many bugs I can squash on the wall even though it is practically impossible for me to see. I listen. I listen to the sound of scurrying insects to know where to strike next. I sit in one spot by the wall to see how many I can kill. I change spots periodically, always avoiding the spider corner because there are webs everywhere there.

I grow tired, but there is no place to sleep. I grow restless, but the stones jab me. So, I listen. I listen for anything. I listen. Then the church bell strikes twelve. Another day.

Chapter 28

Waking, I feel pangs of pain all over my gut. Some are from hunger and others from the stones I passed out on. Growling, my stomach begs for food. Staggering to my feet, I attempt once again to break down the door, but again I fail. Tramping back over to the part of the wall dripping with water, I lick it up until it feels like my tongue is a dirt road trodden over by filthy farmers. Walking back and forth, I listen. I listen for some sign of hope.

I hear nothing besides the creepy crawlers all around me.

What is worse? Being beaten by a whip or starving to death?

I cannot decide.

Walking back and forth, I begin to form impressions in the stones. So, I find my unintentional path with my bare feet; they are so calloused, I cannot feel the stones dig into their soles. Pacing back and forth, I lose count of the bugs that have tried crawling up my leg, so I restart.

I thirst again. I lap up the water on the wall again. I squash bugs again. Then I pace again. It becomes a habit that I lose track of my thoughts. I drain empty. Back and forth. Back and forth. Drink. Squash. Back and Forth.

Blank. Blank like a clean slate. I pace.

I gave up on listening. Listening gets me nowhere. So, I pace.

Creaking.

I think I hear creaking. Turning around, I look at the door with anticipation. A sliver of light breaks into my cellar! Opening, the door lets in a flood of sunshine. Blinded, I cover my eyes only peeking through the cracks between my fingers until my eyes adjust. A silhouette stands at the door. The light wraps around him or her that it looks like it could be an angel coming to save me.

Have I died?

I pat down my body. I am sure I did not die. Unless, even if dead, I can still feel myself.

Stepping out of the light, the silhouette turns out to be my spearman. My dusty smile goes away, but I run towards him anyhow. I will not be left in this dreaded cellar another day. Throwing my arms around his midsection, I refuse to let go unless he takes me outside. I am stuck to him like glue. Running his hands through my mangled hair, he plucks something out of it and presses it between two of his fingers.

"Been in here quite a while, haven't you?" he asks, rubbing his two fingers together.

"I have, and I refuse to be trapped in this bloody cellar another day!" I yell. I wanted to make sure my point was made clear.

Cleaning his ear with his pinky, he nods, "I am getting you out right now. Come with me."

Walking up the flight of steps outside the cellar door, we reach the clearing where the two catapults are nearly complete.

"What happened to Damon's legion?" I ask.

"They slaughtered Austin's men, forcing him to retreat and regroup. Damon's men continued forward and nearly reached the clearing, but at that point an ambush forced him to go back to the east side."

"An ambush led by who?"

"By the people. Austin ran back to the clearing to rally together people to fight, and all under one spirit of passion they rose together overwhelming Damon. That weasel was forced back into his hole."

I nod, but ask, "How did I not hear that?"

"He ran to each house and to each person. Not like he publicly announced it. Plus, the battle itself didn't happen here. I said they got near the clearing."

"Oh, OK," I say. I still don't fully understand why I wouldn't be able to hear the people leaving to confront Damon. Who is to say my spearman can be trusted? I don't trust anyone anymore. Not fully at least.

"What is now expected to occur?" I ask.

"How is your back?"

"Sore, but manageable."

"Then you will be a sneak."

"A sneak?"

"Yes."

"What is that?"

Looking around, my spearman points at each person he sees.

"Everyone needs to eat. Our food supply is running low. Damon has ordered all gates to be shut. Only the east side can receive food from the farmers. So, you need to steal food."

Pointing at myself with a face belonging to one given an impossible mission like to assassinate the king, I stammer, "Me?"

Confused, he replies, "Yes. What seems to be the issue?"

Grabbing my stomach, I say, "I have been starved myself for a long time. I have no energy to expel. Plus, how am I supposed to get food?"

"You will be fed before you leave. You will not be going alone. I shall join you as well as a few other outside farmers who have partnered with us."

"Are all the farmers on our side?"

"No there are some that are loyal to the crown and some who hate both sides and are unpredictable. When we get passed the walls, do not share who we are or our intent. I will do the talking. You are only a mule helping with the carrying."

167

Grunting, I reply, "A mule? Just call me your ass."

"If that is what you prefer," he says sarcastically.

"How are we supposed to get to the farmers?"

Smiling, my spearman replies, "That is the easy part actually. You see there are more than two gates. The North Gate and South Gate are the only gates still in use for trading. However there use to be an East Gate as well as a West Gate. They were discontinued and blocked off with stones."

"How does that help us?"

"Because the West Gate actually used to have a gate house as well. It was not destroyed, the door was only boarded up."

"What you're saying is?"

"We tear away the boarded door and get beyond the wall by climbing through the gate house window."

I nod, trying to figure how I got into this position. My spearman on the other hand is laughing at its genius; I suppose.

"We leave at evening tide, but before then let us eat."

We dine at my spearman's house. His homely wife without teeth and a hairy face that should only belong to a man serves us barley cakes, cooked onions, various legumes, and watered-down beer. She also served us an apple pie to finish it off. Despite the fact she looks like a hairy bear out of hibernation, she is a very good cook.

Evening tide. The time has come. With a cumbersome leather sack on my back that bumps against my legs, I follow behind my spearman who has a leather sack as well. It stretches far down to the top of his thighs and is wider than his body. Mine is slightly smaller, but not by much. I am going to struggle to carry any vegetables depending how full he intends to stuff my sack. Reaching the end of the west side, we come to the former gate house. A stack of warped lumber is piled next to it. Someone already must have taken down the door for us. Trotting inside the stone room, we kick up a cloud of

168

dust. Coughing, I cover my mouth with the sleeve of the smelly tunic my spearman gave me. He sheared the bottom of it to accommodate my short legs. Cobwebs clutter the ceiling, intertwining like a mistress weaved them together for the purpose of clothing the ceiling. Looking to my left, I spot the window that used to be used to speak with travelers and tradesmen before they entered the city. Now it is just an empty hole in the wall.

Throwing our leather sacks out the window first, we clamber over the edge. Slipping them back on, we slink into the darkness given cover by a canopy of trees. The extra darkness they provide makes me think they are actually rebels themselves reaching their arms over our heads to protect us. Tramping through the woods, I try to watch my step so I don't step on too many twigs or leaves. Every noise makes me jump. Imagining soldiers behind every tree, I get chills whenever something moves. Of course, it's only animals like badgers and birds, but my imagination says otherwise. Reaching the end of the forest, we come to a pitted dirt path. Fields surround it.

"Do you know your way around here?" I ask.

My spearman nods, replying, "Yes. Follow my lead."

Stepping onto the path, he walks briskly. I struggle to keep up with him, having to skip every fifth step to make up the distance. Fields are all I see besides the occasional shack in which farmer's family lives. Everything is silent and quiet. The countryside is asleep, but the stars watch us intently, shining their bright lights upon us so they don't miss a step we take. Coming across another shack, this one with a black lamb tied out front by the door, we come to a halt. Stalking closer, we come to the door. Knocking in a rhythmic pattern, my spearman waits for a response. Another knock from inside repeating the same pattern replies. Then my spearman raps the door three more times. It opens. The keeper! We're at the keeper's homestead. It just struck me now that his shack is bigger than the others we passed.

Moving his blond hair to the side, he looks at my spearman with his dreamy blue eyes. The keeper's thin lips twitch and his hands shake like at any moment he is going to draw a sword.

"When is breakfast served?" he asks in a hushed voice.

"At the dawn of freedom," my spearman replies.

"Welcome, brother. Please fill your sacks quickly. I will every night, from now on, drop off a portion of pulse at the west gate house. I needed confirmation tonight, and my little boy has an awful fever. I fear for his well-being." Shaking his head, he continues, "Never mind that. Please fill your sacks. What you need is behind my place."

"Thank you, brother. My prayers go out to your boy as well."

"Bless you. Now go."

Closing the door on us, the keeper goes inside.

"Don't dawdle now," my spearman says, running behind the shack. Crates of goods ranging from barley to potatoes face us. Even a few freshly picked apples are available to us.

"Fill your sack so that you have the maximum you can carry," my spearman says. Picking one of everything, I begin filling my sack with potatoes, barley, onions, leeks, and apples. I fill my sack till it is a little over half way filled. Slinging it over my back, I hunch over. I feel like I am carrying the carcass of a cow.

"We must hurry. Let's go," my spearman whispers. Running off towards the woods we came out of, we scurry through the night. The beaten farm road nearly breaks my ankles every time I step into a divot or a pothole. I fall several times, like I am trying to run up a rocky mountain.

After I scrape my knee, again, my spearman snaps at me, "Pick your feet up, boy. A guard comes through here around this time."

"That wasn't disclosed to me earlier," I growl, struggling to my feet. Sweating, I pant like a dog.

"We're nearly there," my spearman says.

To our right, I can see the wooded area. I also hear the stamping of hooves. Turning around, I spot a guard carriage. Two guards sit in the back of the carriage as another steers the horse. My throat constricts. The one steering the horse spots us and points. I hear him yell something.

"Hurry!" my spearman shouts. We bolt for the woods. The stamping of hooves increases in pace. The guards shout at us to stop. Running faster and faster, the woods get closer and closer. Tripping over a root, I fall onto my face. Scrambling to my feet, I try to catch up to my spearman who is already at the tree line. The sound of stamping hooves ends with the screeching of wheels. Shouting, the guards dismount from their carriage. They come running for us. Crossing the tree line, I dash for the glade. The shouting increases in volume. Sweat beads across my forehead and my arms feel clammy. Heaving in deep breaths, I feel my saliva thicken. I lost sight of my spearman. Coming to the glade, I jut over to the left into the thickest part of the forest. Briars and thorns tear at my flesh. Biting my tongue, I try to keep silent. Only low grunts escape my lips. Diving into a thicket of bushes, I drop my sack and lie on the ground.

I don't see the guards, but I do hear them talking among themselves. Steadying my breathing, I swallow the lump of sticky saliva stuck in my throat.

Hope those weasels don't find me, I think to myself. The guards quit talking. I hear their footsteps go in different directions.

Did they split up?

I peek through the little break between the two bushes I lie behind. I see nobody. A twig snaps behind me. Nearly jumping out of my tunic, I let out a yelp. I hear a guard come to a halt.

No. No.

I close my eyes and pray they don't find me. Getting closer, the footsteps get louder. Crawling backwards, I rise onto my knees. I can see a pair of legs in the distance. It is now or never. Jumping to my feet, I sprint in the opposite direction.

"Over here!" I hear a guard shout. Tumbling through the thicker side of the forest, I feel so clumsy. Hundreds of branches, dozens of bushes, and millions of thorns reach out for me to bring me down. The trees once on my side have now turned on me like they were spies the entire time. Ducking underneath a branch, I don't notice a rock at my feet. Flipping in the air, I land on my back, gasping for another breath. The scabs across my back are wet with blood. Letting out a war whoop, the guard chasing me has saliva drooling down his stubby chin. Drawing his sword, he jumps at me. Fire burns in his eyes like a mountain lion attacking its prey. Piercing through the air, an arrow hits the guard in the shoulder, throwing him to the side. Wailing in pain, he tries to get back up, but another arrow hits him in the throat. Dropping his sword, he breathes his last.

Staying crouched, I look around. I don't see anybody. I hear someone running. Standing up to see who it is, I see that the footsteps belong to the two other guards with swords already drawn. Scurrying away, I break back into the glade. Running without the sack on my back makes me feel ten times faster. The guards, though, are not far behind. Making it out of the thick stuff, they are right on my tail. Jumping out in front of me, a figure catches me off guard. Trying to get out of the way, I trip over my own feet, falling prostrate on the ground. Turning over onto my back, I see that it is a man with blond hair. Pulling back a bow, he fires an arrow hitting one of the two guards beneath his shoulder pad. Falling over, the guard lets out a cry. One guard remains. Pulling the last arrow out of his quiver, the archer draws again. Firing his last arrow, he misses by a hair as the guard bobs to the left. Throwing his bow onto the ground, the archer draws his sword and charges the guard. I sit up at an angle that doesn't hurt my back as much.

172

Clashing blades together, the soldier and the strange archer throw each other back. Walking in circles around each other, I can see faintly who the archer is even through the darkness. It looks like Frederick, the keeper. Swinging first, the guard goes for Frederick's head. Ducking, he jabs at the guard's side, but the guard blocks Frederick's blade by swinging his sword in a circle. Blocking each other's blows, they evenly match each other until Frederick grabs the guard's arm, the one with sword in hand, and slices the poor weasel's arm right off at the elbow. Clutching his arm as it's gushing blood, the guard lets out a wail before Frederick comes down at the weasel's neck, beheading him.

Throwing his hair out of his face, Frederick looks at me with his blade in one hand and the dead weasel's arm in the other. Both drip with blood. I look back at him. He breathes heavily.

"Go," he says. I nod, running for my life as I hear the church bell strike twelve.

Chapter 29

"You left me for dead!" I scream at my spearman. It is mid-afternoon, and the sun is high in the sky. I was looking for him all morning and could not find him till I spotted him at his house drinking a glass of water. Enraged, I could feel every vein inside me swell. I think I even caused my spearman's water to evaporate a little bit I was that hot with rage.

Seemingly indifferent, maybe even amused, my spearman replies, "What do you mean 'left for dead?' You were supposed to keep up with me."

"That is outrageous, you no good bastard. How do you expect me to keep up with you, especially with my stature?" I ask, pointing at my chest.

Laughing, he says, "I don't, boy. I expect nothing. I only hoped you would help me with that one expedition to prove yourself."

"Prove myself?"

"Yes, otherwise you are quite useless, I must say. I mean, you don't got brains to build a catapult. Don't have the muscle to lift rocks. You can't even fight well, much less run."

Boiling over with anger, I pull at my hair, gnashing my teeth.

Laughing even harder, my spearman pours the rest of his water on my head, saying, "Cool down, boy. Look hotter than the blasted sun."

"I hate you," I snap back. Water runs down the side of my face, dripping from my dirty blond hair.

"I can put you back in that cellar if you would like that better."

"Oh, pierce the hogshead with your doxy, bastard."

Slapping me across my mouth, my spearman growls, "Watch your tone with me, powder boy. This is not The Manor. I will take measures into my own hands if must be."

Rubbing my jaw, I snarl back, "Killing me would be a blessing."

"Don't tempt me," he says, tossing his glass on the ground so it shatters into a million pieces.

"I wouldn't dare," I say as I stomp away.

"You don't run these parts, boy!" he shouts.

I ignore him.

At the opening where the catapults are, I wander around. They are practically complete. A few finishing touches are being put in place at the very top of the two structures as a couple men are at their peaks working on them. They hammer and chisel carefully as they hold onto wood planks to stay balanced so as not to fall. Calming down, I begin to breathe normally again. I no longer feel like I am penning a lion inside of me. Instead, I feel like all the anger inside me broke out from behind the dam it was trapped behind.

"They found out! They found out!" the messenger boy cries, running down the main street leading towards the catapults. Those on top of them look up at the boy.

"They found out! They found out!"

Stepping out of the surrounding houses, and leaving their jobs, people stream into the miniature city-square to see what the messenger boy has to say. His long hair bounces in his ecstatic eyes as he waves his fist around.

"Who found out what?" asks a bearded man on top of one of the catapults.

"Them weasels know about the produce being smuggled into our side of the city!" he replies.

"How?"

"A wounded weasel reported it to General Damon."

"What?" Looking over my shoulder, I spot my spearman saying, "How did the soldiers know it was us? How did they get wounded?" he says looking at me with a glare, he marches in my direction, "what happened out there last night?"

Stammering, I struggle to find the words to say, "I— I don't know—I thought they were all dead."

"Dead? You were supposed to hide and escape, not kill them!"

"They saw us."

"They didn't know it was us."

"How do you know?"

Scowling, he rubs his face, "I just do. How did you kill them?"

Scratching my neck, I look at the disfigured cobblestone beneath my feet replying, "I didn't."

"Then who did?"

Clearing my throat, I whisper, "Frederick."

"Frederick! He is our main supplier. If they know it was him, we are going to starve," my spearman says, pulling at his black hair. It's like he's mourning over the dead.

"It wasn't like I asked him to help," I protest.

"If you weren't such a short little bastard you could have outrun those weasels. It is your fault."

"What is this all about?" asks Austin, who broke past the wall of people surrounding us.

Running up to Austin, the messenger boy skids to a stop, proclaiming, "The weasels know about last night and about Frederick."

Nodding, Austin keeps a straight face, one that hides both anger and concern. Pacing back and forth, Austin investigates the sky, pondering what he just heard, and rubbing the stubble on his chin. Rougher around the edges, Austin must feel the wear and tear of revolution. No one says a word. My spearman is the first to break the silence.

"Austin, why are you here and not with your men?" he asks. The expression on his face is the same expression I had as a child when trying to get out of trouble by changing the topic of discussion.

Coming to a halt, Austin clears his throat and faces my spearman.

"Excuse me, what did you say?" he asks.

Hesitating, my spearman pulls at his collar, repeating his question, "Your men, aren't you supposed to be with them?"

Nodding, Austin seems to be musing over what my spearman asked, "Indeed, I am."

Grinning, my spearman relaxes saying, "You really surprised us arriving so early."

Backhanding my spearman, Austin kicks out his legs, forcing him to kneel snarling, "Learn some respect, you stubborn ass. I did not come down here for a social call and to make your acquaintance. I came here to punish who is to blame for the massacre about to occur."

Raising his hands in front of his face, my spearman trembles like a crippled man trying to stand, asking, "What do you mean, master?"

"A spy told me that Damon is preparing a band of soldiers, not for the sake of raiding us, but rather for our suppliers. Was it not you who led last night's expedition?"

"Sir—"

"Was it not?"

"Yes."

Drawing his sword, Austin pinches the blade between his index finger and thumb saying, "I have depended upon many like you. That comes with trust. You have failed to uphold that trust."

"Please, don't kill me. Please. I beg you," my spearman weeps, bowing before Austin like he would be worshipping a god.

Smug, Austin smiles at my spearman's submission as he rubs his fingers up and down his blade.

"What reason do I have to spare you?" he asks.

178

"Because of my loyalty."

Laughing, Austin asks, "Are you loyal?"

"Yes, as you say I will do. I will not raise my voice against you."

"I like the sound of that." Sheathing his sword, Austin kneels in front of my spearman, raising his head. Looking into my spearman's eyes, Austin lights up with a mischievous gleam. Chuckling, Austin says, "Let your silence be your testament." Pulling out a double-edged dagger from his black cloak he says, "Open your mouth."

"No! No!" my spearman cries, scuffling backwards. Knocking him on his back, Austin pins my spearman's arms against the ground. Four of Austin's men come to his side, holding down my spearman's legs and opening his mouth.

Turning away, I shove my fingers inside my ears. Even with my fingers deep in my ear canals, I can hear my spearman gurgle and screech.

Austin must be The Beast, I think to myself.

Chapter 30

Massacre. That is the only word available. King Oscar did not hold back a punishment towards the farmers involved with Austin. Burning their fields, slaughtering their livestock, and murdering their families. The head of every farmer along with their families figured to be in cahoots with Austin were stuck on pikes so that their faces look towards the west side of the city. Just another jab at Austin. The farmers who survived have excommunicated the rebels. It would be easier to climb a mountain than to persuade the farmers to aid the revolution. No one blames them, but the rebels are now on borrowed time.

Hungry and enraged, Austin is tired of waiting. When fire is played with, more than one person gets burned. Morning of a new day, the day after last night's massacre, Austin along with his men surround the catapults. They are ready. Pulling himself onto the base of both catapults, Austin looks like a tattered war hero — stubble upon his chin, dirt on his clothes, sweat on his brow, and fire in his eyes. He is a handsome man on the outside, but he is a demon on the inside.

"We have far too long been submitting to a powder boy over in The Manor who has burned our fields and killed our people. Justice is ours to fulfill," he says with great tenacity. "They are The Beast. They are the ones to be killed. Let us raise our voices. Let us rise above our adversaries. Let us crush our enemies!" he cries with a loud war whoop. Everyone cheers along with him, carrying on loudly. "Let us strike back!" Jumping off the catapult, Austin motions for his men to load the catapults. The giant brutes, with guts the size of a full grown steer, roll the stones into the catapults.

"Let them feel justice!" Austin shouts.

Swinging through the air, both catapults launch their large boulders towards the sky. I see the rocks get smaller and smaller and soon lose them behind the buildings.

"Again! Do not stop!" Austin cries.

Pulling down the arm and bucket, men strain to reset the catapult. My spearman is one of those men. As soon as the arm is set in position, the brutes quickly load two more rocks into the catapults. As the boulders soar through the air, the audience surrounding the catapults watches with amusement. Cheering, many of them beg for more stones to fly. Austin continues to holler commands, and dozens of boulders are launched. Grunting, heaving, and pushing, the men load the catapults sweating like pigs.

"They will be coming at any moment. Men, guard our square and strengthen our barricades."

Overnight, Austin had his forces position themselves so they could be prepared for today. He also set up barricades across the roads with rocks, baskets, wagons, and any other items the people gave away to be used. Now the streets are filled with random trash and lines of rebels waiting for their opportunity. Archers stand on top of buildings, prepared for any sort of attack. The sound of creaking lumber, rushing wind, and cheering people clouds the air around me. Suddenly the inside of an abandoned cellar doesn't sound like a bad resting place. A nagging headache begins to eat away at the back of my head.

An hour must have gone by, and not a single soldier cared to stop the rebels. No one came by.

"Sir, no more rocks are available," says one of Austin's men.

"We will find more another day. What is this? Damon too much of a coward to drop by?" Austin asks, scowling. Walking around the catapults, he scratches his head and rubs his stubble. Spitting into the ground, he kicks up a few pebbles with his feet.

"Austin!" calls a rebel.

"What?" he calls back.

"Someone is here to talk with you."

Strutting towards Austin with a white flag in hand, a soldier, bigger than Goliath wears no helmet. He is stone faced. His strong figure, one that belongs to a general, does not shudder as rebels close around him spitting and screaming. Austin, laughing, approaches the soldier mimicking his behavior.

"So serious, are we? Surrendering, are we?" he taunts.

Remaining silent, the soldier, two times the size of Austin, stands still like a statue.

Raising an eyebrow and running his hand through his slimy long hair, Austin smiles, "Silent? Such an accomplishment for a weasel. Does the pain of lost bite you?"

Unrolling a scroll, an official scroll from the king with fine red ribbons on the side, the soldier reads, "King Oscar, commander of the Royal Guard," the rebels laugh with contempt and, ignoring them, the soldier continues, "head of The Royal Union has officially declared war against the peasants of the west side." Finishing, the soldier hands the scroll over to Austin.

Turning red, Austin shakes the scroll like a bone for a dog, "You have the audacity to cross enemy lines to feed me this?" Shoving the scroll in the soldier's face, Austin rips at his own hair, breathing heavily between his barred teeth. Then he breaks out laughing like a jester. Grabbing his sides, he picks the scroll up and asks, "What are the rules of war again? Remind me."

Unshaken, the soldier replies with his low rumbling voice, "If I was to remind you the rules of war, I would be under the assumption you were once aware of the rules. Obviously, by the sackcloth you wear, you have never set foot on an actual battleground. So, the code of conduct a soldier follows would not apply to you, a low, sordid plebeian. I will not waste my time with a filthy rebel. Just understand that war gives King Oscar every right to hang each and every one of you as prisoners of war."

Snarling, Austin crumbles the scroll with his veiny hands. Seething with anger, he stomps over to a wood pile out by one of the many broken down homes in the clearing. Ripping the axe out of the biggest log, he drags it back to where he stood. Not flinching, the soldier just watches.

"I guess you're right. I have never been taught chivalry. I never read the rules of war."

"Attack me if you dare. Just know that it will not save you from King Oscar."

Raising the axe in both hands, Austin taps the wooden handle with his talons. Laughing again, he shakes his shaggy head, "No. Your death alone will not save us. The Beast wants the hearts of the real enemy."

Frowning, the soldier knits his eyebrows, "The Beast?"

Nodding, Austin replies, "Yes. Now someone get Mother."

Several people run to fetch Crow Mother. Laying his hand on his hilt, the soldier asks, "What black magic have you delved into?"

Laughing, Austin says, "I have only called upon the audible voice in my ear. The one King Oscar called foolish and the one Jonah called evil. I call it power. True power. King Oscar is an ear pleaser, merely a king of people. I am a god."

The sky darkens with crows. The cackling of black demon birds makes my ears hurt. Parting, the crowd of jeering rebels fall silent as Crow Mother comes near. Her hooded cloak casts a shadow over her face which is a blessing in disguise because if anyone were to see her real face, they would be white-washed with horror. Squirming, the soldier wraps his entire hand around his sword. His focus is on Crow Mother as his back faces Austin.

"An enemy?" questions Crow Mother coming to a halt. Her crow army perches around the clearing.

"Yes, Mother," Austin replies.

Looking the soldier up and down, she nods. "A fine one, too. Much larger than a mammoth." Coming closer, Crow Mother reaches out for his shoulder.

Drawing his Viking size sword, the soldier raises it above his head shouting, "If you lay a hand on me, I will remove it!"

Breaking his back, Austin wedges his axe between the soldier's spine. Austin laughs at the soldier's weakness, kicking him like a dying dog.

"Such a pity," says Crow Mother, "I suppose it is only right we feed him to the birds."

Cackling, all the crows swoop down at once like a black tidal wave. They peck, they screech, they fight over the soldier's wiggling body. Blood-curdling cries rip through the air. Tears well up in my eyes. It is horrific. Blood spills across the cobblestone. Crow Mother cackles. Devouring the soldier, the birds leave nothing behind except bone.

Chapter 31

Official war has changed Austin's approach to his entire revolution. No longer is he planning small thrown together raids, but instead he is planning actual battle strategies. Gathering together all his men around the catapults, he splits them all into four units, appointing certain individuals above them. Then devising an attack, he sends those four units into different areas on the west side. According to him, his next plan of attack is to break through King Oscar's wall of men defending the east side of the city. Austin also mentions how all the men on the east side besides certain wealthy people are now soldiers. The women and children have found refuge among the farmers, so catapult attacks will not be as effective.

However, for me this is kind of a good thing. No longer does anyone seem to expect me to do anything. Many men, women, and even children have a purpose and do not bother to ask me what I am doing because they themselves are far too busy. My spearman no longer has time to watch over me either. He is far too busy serving Austin in one of the four units. Of course, with so much freedom I have been plotting my escape. Being ignored means I also struggle to get food and even water. I feel famished. Most would assume escaping at night would be best because it is dark and everyone is asleep, but that is when every street is filled with at least one watchman if not more. So, if I was to attempt an escape at night I would undoubtedly be caught.

During the day everyone is awake. That does not mean anyone notices me. The hardest part will still be the rebel units. I have a faint idea where Austin positioned them, but I cannot be sure. If any of them catch me trying to sneak away, I will most likely be killed for treason. Yet at the rate I am going, I will starve if I don't try to escape sooner or later. Fleeing through the gate my spearman and I used may be an option, but ever since we used it rebels have been guarding it in case Damon decides to use it as well. Unless I create a diversion. Having no allies, I cannot depend upon others to help me create a distraction. It would all have to be on my own. The only way to figure out how to do so is to inspect the gate house.

Looking around the clearing, I check for anyone who may be watching me. No one. Running off, I head for the West Gate House. It takes me a few minutes before I see it. Getting closer, I walk pretending I am looking for someone.

"Mary! Mary!" I shout. At the gate house guarding the door are three rebels. They all wear iron breastplates (Austin being a blacksmith taught a few people how to make basic armor and weapons) as well as leather helmets which only cover their heads and do nothing to protect their faces. They all have spears and wooden shields. Nothing that stands out as military grade, but against an unarmed kid would do hefty damage. Especially a kid with ribs that can be seen through his skin.

"Boy, what are you doing?" asks the shortest of the three. He has a round, fat face that reminds me of a eunuch. His voice is higher than a lady's, and his helmet is two sizes too big. Definitely a new recruit.

"Looking for a girl I know," I reply. They all look at each other then back at me.

"We haven't seen anyone for the past hour," the fat face one replies, "especially a woman."

"Haven't seen a woman since this blasted revolution started," says the tallest of the three. He has a shield that is only big enough to cover his face and a spear with a handle that has a crack going all the way up it. The middle rebel looks no better. They all must be new recruits.

"What I would pay for a strumpet," says the middle rebel licking his thick lips. If I ever saw a human wolf, today is the day. I fear to see the middle rebel when there is a full moon out.

"Say, when we win this blasted war, why don't we all grab a woman, some mead, and find a place for the night?" says the fat face one.

"I like the way you talk," says the wolf man, nudging the fat face one.

Looking at me, the tallest of the three asks, "How does this Mary you look for appear?"

"How does she look?" I ask.

"Aye."

Thinking quickly, I reply, "She is a fine dame. If I were of marrying age, I would certainly take her as my wife. None compare to her."

The three men nod with excitement. Wolf man wets his lips, saying, "Don't worry. If we find her, we'll let you know."

"Thank you."

"Is she of age?" asks the fat face one.

"Certainly. She is full in figure and has immaculate breasts." They all slap each other on the back, laughing. "Please tell me if you find her," I say, trying to sound concerned.

"We will," replies the fat face one.

All I know is if a Mary does actually come along, she will be defiled before they say a word to me. Walking away, I can still hear them talking about Mary. I have my diversion planned out. It may be easier than I thought. If those men are craving a woman, they will run at the sound of her name. Finding an abandoned stone house, I stand at the doorstep. I am still close enough to the gate house for myself to be heard, but far enough away so that I can run around the buildings on this street and sneak outside past the wall. Smiling to myself, I feel proud for how clever I am.

"Mary, there you are!" I shout purposely loud, "I am so glad I found you! Please stay here now, I need to get you something! I will be right back!" I quickly run away, hoping my plan worked. Sprinting behind the stone houses, I come back to the street leading to the gate house. The three rebels are gone. Running towards their imagined Mary, I see they took their weapons with them. They have certainly not seen a woman in a long time. Jumping through the window in the gate house, I scamper off into the woods I remember so painfully well.

What if the guards kill me? Or what if the farmers recognize my face and slaughter me? I think to myself as I barrel through the forest. I never considered that. I could certainly be seen as a traitor. Maybe I'll be hanged! Stopping, I bend over sucking in quick, sharp breaths. *They may even have orders to kill me on account of treason. Especially how I ran out on my father.* Looking back, I know it is too late to return to the rebels. My only chance is to confront the guards. Unless I run for another kingdom, but I don't know how to get to any other kingdoms. *What about Liberty?* I certainly cannot travel to Liberty. They are our enemies. Unless that was all fake because by now Liberty should have been here. Unless our forces are just that strong. I doubt it. Doctor Commons used to say King Oscar is a brilliant liar.

Sweating, I wipe my brow with my arm.

No turning back, I think to myself. Running forward, I get to the glade. I remember so vividly how Frederick saved my life. According to Austin, Frederick is dead. I'm not sure how accurate that is. I didn't see his head on one of the pikes. If Austin is right, that means there is no keeper. He said King Oscar no longer gives the farmers representation in the government because of their

190

disobedience. Not like they had much representation to begin with.

Closing my eyes, I take in deep, methodical, breaths. Clear my head. Clear my thoughts. Clear my fears.

Breaking out from the forest, I open my eyes to the familiar country road. Guards march up and down it as others ride on carriages. Waving my arms in the air like a flightless bird, I cry out for help. A guard near the forest looks up at me, drawing his sword immediately. Falling onto my face before the guard, I weep. I cry so that he may help me. I cry so that I can let it all out. Everything I have witnessed.

Mostly death. Doctor Commons. More death.

Waving over a carriage, he lifts me into it and brings me back into the city. Wiping my tears, I stay lying in the back of the carriage. The east side was never so inviting. We are heading towards The Manor. Stopping, the driver of the carriage orders me out of it. Leading me to The Manor's entrance, he orders the guards to open the gate. Walking inside, he leads me to where my father's house is. Boulders scatter the inside of The Manor. The quaint homes made for generals, Royal Union members, and other highly regarded soldiers are now devastated. Rocks crush the many beautiful flowers that used to look at the sun with elation. Boulders have wedged themselves into the walls of many homes that now have cracked or crumbled. It looks like the heavens released boulder-size hail. The true miracle is that my father's house looks untouched, like the rocks knew they couldn't even get near it.

"Go inside, I will bring General Damon here soon," the driver says. I comply. Sitting down by my father's kitchen table, I remember so well how my father threw a knife at me. How I nearly died several times here. Nothing sticks in my mind better than those memories when I sit at this table. Opening the door, my father steps inside

191

wearing his full iron armor. A simple grin resides on his face.

"You mean those goddamn peasants did not kill you? I was sure they would," he says. I shake my head. "Must have been hell. What are they like on the other side?"

"Different," I reply.

Chuckling, he rubs his stubble just like Austin would, saying, "Those dim-witted bastards will get what they deserve after I am through with them. It was considerate of them to at least leave my place unscathed."

"What do you have planned?" I ask.

"You never do learn. When have I ever shared battle strategies with you? That is private information."

He's acting differently. He's talking differently. Everything is funny to him right now. My stern, cutthroat, ruthless father never showed so much humor.

"What is going on?" I ask.

"What do you mean?" he asks, scratching his face. A large lump like a molehill sticks out from the top of his head.

"You seem to be acting strange," I say.

Laughing, he finds himself a drink he left on the table. A glass of strong drink. Taking a swig, he swirls it in his hand chuckling, "Strange, you say. I suppose this may seem peculiar."

"It is."

"Have you ever been struck by a flying rock? Have you? Have you, boy? Have you?" he asks. I search for a smile, I wait for a chuckle, but none follow.

"No."

"Have you ever dealt with an ass as a king who threatens you every day that if one more person dies, then you will too? I stare at those heads on those pikes not knowing if mine will follow suit! You understand that, boy?!" he bellows, slamming his glass on the table, splashing his brown drink all over the floor.

Shaking my head, I whisper, "No."

"I did not think so. Do not think my seemingly different demeanor is for you. If you died today or the day you were born, I would not even shed a tear. Your mother died on your account, and next time you address me, call me 'sir.'"

I nod, hiding my face from his. To hide the leaking tear out of the corner of my eye.

"Stay out of trouble and away from that riff-raff in the west."

"Yes, sir."

Leaving, my father mumbles something to himself. I watch him close the door, hearing him chuckle again.

Chapter 32

Lying in bed, I sleep most of the morning away. Normally at this time, on a regular day, I would be with Doctor Commons. We would help patients as he shares his wisdom with me. Watering his dying flowers or making food, he would always ask for my help or just for my presence. I had no friends besides him. I still have nightmares regarding his death. Sleep is only a cistern of horrors awaiting to be drunk from.

Wet with tears, my pillow becomes unbearable to lie on. Smearing the remaining drops on my cheeks with the back of my scarred hand, I lie my head on the mattress. I have no one to turn to and no one to befriend. Embracing this truth, I remain indoors, not allowing the outside to pollute me anymore. Stiff, my body refuses to move. My back cramps up and my legs go limp. I have not let my body relax in a long time. Not since I became Austin's prisoner. It's a new sensation my body is struggling to handle. Maybe when mid-day arrives, I will force myself to eat something, though I feel no hunger. I feel desolate. Empty. Broken.

Hours pass by. I don't sleep. My mind is tortured; I cannot sleep. So, I cry. Mostly. Or I recall all my troubles which make me angry, just to remember Doctor Commons and cry all over again. It's a bitter cycle. An unbroken one. It has repeated itself all morning. No one has come by to help assuage me. My father is down with his men preparing for their next battle along with everyone else who didn't evacuate the city. A city split in two. Divided over a figurative monster. One that lurks in the mind of man according to Jonah who once again has disappeared.

Yet I can't help but think that The Beast was merely a reason for the people to rebel. Maybe there always was a seething bitterness towards King Oscar unknown to me. Up until Austin claimed the west side as his own, I always thought our city's state was fine. Maybe not perfect, but good enough to maintain itself. Apparently not. Apparently, I misjudged how strong the tension was between the throne and its people. What is to occur if Austin succeeds? Will it return to normal? Or will it not? Daunting questions cast a gloomy shadow over me and the kingdom's entire future.

Finally, through beating myself with answerless questions, I force my legs to move. They rebuke me, lashing me with soreness, but I fight through it. My rigid back will not allow me to bend over, but it cannot stop me from standing. Every bone in my body crackles when I stretch towards the sky. Stiffness and soreness encase me like a cocoon, but I have spent far too much time in bed. Lumbering into the kitchen, I hear my stomach growl at me. It finally realizes it needs food. Searching through the cupboards, I come across nothing but bread. My father must not be eating much. Now that I think about it, he did look skinnier yesterday. Living off alcohol most likely.

Grabbing the bread, I eat it as is. It is not very satisfying, but it is enough to keep my stomach quiet. Meandering through the house, I hum in hope to block out the thoughts and memories in my head. It also keeps me from boredom. Leaving the house would give me something to do, but I fear everyone. There is no trust among people anymore. At least I don't trust people anymore. How can I? Everyone who was ever good to me died at the hands of monsters. Some on my behalf, such as my mother.

196

Closing my eyes, I erase that thought. My father has ingrained in me a sense of blame. Blame I cast on myself. Blame I want to get rid of. Pacing the kitchen, I feel much better physically, but not mentally. I still feel like a prisoner. Like the crows overhead are watching me so that Austin knows where I am. Crow Mother is always watching. Shuddering, I pace faster. Faster I go until I get too dizzy to walk straight. Sitting down, I cry some more. Everything seems bleak. Everything *is* bleak.

Chapter 33

Awaking, I get out of bed immediately. Not because I have any big plans, but rather to hopefully escape the vicious cycle I fell into yesterday. Eating a breakfast consisting of bread, I walk outside. The sun blinds me, forcing me to block my eyes with my hand. Silence. Never before has The Manor been so silent. It is almost peaceful. Except that means everyone is preparing for war, the opposite of peace. Wearing a simple black tunic which cooks me in the sun, I take a stroll to The Manor's exit. Nobody is around. There are no guards. There are no men of royalty. Nobody. Looking around, I play a game with myself, trying to find the most interesting spots boulders have lodged themselves into. Some were stuck into the wall surrounding the open court while others had taken out statues. However, the most interesting spot I found a boulder was on top of a chimney. It somehow landed that half of its body went into the chimney and the other half stuck out of it. The most surprising thing was that the chimney remained intact.

Finally reaching the exit, I find my way to the glade that leads to The Manor's entrance. The Manor remains wide open so that anybody can go in and out as they please. They must have been in a hurry to escape. Reaching the end of the glade, I look at the cobblestone street before me and consider whether or not I really want to go any further. I know the east side well, but I do not want to run into a war zone. Yet being trapped inside, bored, sounds just as bad.

Glancing back at The Manor, I proceed forward. I know city-square is not safe. I must stay away from the main road that cuts through the east side as well since that is the road of transportation for soldiers. It is best to stay on small alleyways. Slinking through the streets, I manage to clear my head. Throwing stones, going in and out of homes freely, I find more boulders. Not as close together as in The Manor, but they are still around. A few buildings fell into ash due to them. Not many, however. Walking, I realize I am getting closer to The Pit. Crows circle the sky, swooping down every once and awhile like black bolts of lightning. Rounding the street corner, I see the two drunks. They are bigger than the last time I saw them. Drinking from jugs, they let the crummy fluid run all over their scruffy faces. Uglier than rats, they dig into the loose, stony dirt with their same old shovels, but their cart is nowhere to be seen. Yet it must be pointless considering they have a pile of bodies beside them that would require three or four carts. Rotting away, the corpses become food for the crows which fight over every scrap of meat. Seemingly unaware, the two drunks dig talking among themselves.

"Damn, rebels making sky fell," says the short one.

"The sky didn't fall," protests the other. Their voices are deeper and throatier, like they are gargling marbles.

"Ain't serious. Some figure of talk or something."

"Don't talk stupid. Ain't much for your thinkin'."

"What you talkin' about?"

"This ain't no fun. Look at all these men. Smelling like the plague."

"So?"

The taller drunk slaps the short one over the head, making him kick his jug of whiskey over.

"Dammit," the short one mutters, picking his jug up and setting it right at his feet again.

"Stop jabbering. We ain't got all day to dig," the taller one grumbles, throwing another pile of dirt to the side.

The shorter one picks up a body off the pile, throwing it in the hole they made. Covering the body like it is just a dead horse, they go onto the next one.

"The Pit short of room," says the shorter one.

"Burn 'em soon," says the taller one.

They continue to dig, slapping each other on occasions and taking swigs from their brown jugs. I watch in horror. Dozens of people are stacked on top of each other, lifeless. The stench is so pungent I can smell it from where I am standing. I have no clue how the crows can continue to feast off their bodies. They must be mental.

"Should started this long time ago," says the shorter one, examining the pile of bodies.

"Aye," replies the taller one, wiping his forehead. "Damn rebels, they ain't got no control."

"Aye. Bloody fools. Ain't any as smart as us two."

"Say that again."

"I ain't gonna say nothin'. Get to work," the taller one snaps, shoveling again.

What madness is this? They treat these bodies with no respect. Stumbling around drunk, they throw the corpses around and toss dirt wherever they please. They even feed the crows pieces of flesh when they are bored. Kicking his jug over again, the shorter one bends over to pick it up. While straightening his back, he spots me. Smiling, he flashes his remaining yellow.

"Aye. Ain't you familiar?" he asks.

The taller one puts down his shovel, looking at me. His eyes are squinted. Nodding, he replies, "I think he Damon son."

"The big weasel?" The shorter one asks with big eyes.

Slapping the back of his head, the taller one growls, "I said he ain't no weasel. He some sort of royal sort."

Rubbing his head, the shorter one asks, "What he doin' here?"

"Ask."

"What you doin' here?"

Silent, I blink in reply. I don't know them and don't know whether I should reply or not.

"Think he deaf?" asks the shorter one.

Shaking his head, the taller one coughs in his hand. Rubbing his palm all over his face, he says, "No. He is shy."

"Should I offer him a drink?"

"Ask."

"Boy, you wanna swig?" Lifting his jug, the shorter one waves it in the air like I'm a dog.

Shaking my head, I stand still. Everything about them, about The Pit, reeks. I don't want to get near them much less take a drink from their jugs.

"He ain't a social sort," comments the shorter one, scratching his scruffy face.

Slapping the shorter one over the head as he takes a swig, the taller one laughs at his friend, choking over his drink. Looking at me, the taller one asks, "Ain't ya' the one that ran? Ain't rebels make you their ass?"

I nod my head. I have taken a few steps back. I hope to escape soon.

"Don't fear us," says the shorter one elbowing the taller one in the side. "We ain't out for ya', just burying fellows."

"To The Pit they go," jokes the taller one, crossing his arms like he is prepared to be embalmed. Then falling over onto the dirt, he spills his jug which he put down behind himself. "Curses," he mutters, wiping down his ratty tunic with his hand like it's a towel. Picking up his jug, he fumbles with it, trying to wipe off the dirt. Shrugging, he takes another swig, nearly falling over on his back again.

"Clumsy," teases the shorter one, pointing as he laughs.

Getting up, the taller one clobbers the shorter one in the gut with his jug, making him gasp. Then growling, the taller one says, "Get to work."

"Fine," says the shorter one, still wrapping his arms around his gut.

Looking at me, the taller one chuckles, "Beware the Beast. Blasted loonies," he snorts, turning around.

Running, I get away as quickly as I can before they decide to say anymore. It may be wrong to hate a simple minded fellow, but I hate them. I hate them.

Chapter 34

Waking up in my familiar bed inside Doctor Commons' old house, I sit up straight. Nothing has changed from the last time I saw the place. It still has broken medicine bottles everywhere and none of the furniture is where it belongs, but the nostalgic feel of sleeping again in his house is enough for me to relive the memories I had here. The good ones. Fresh, dewy tears came to my eyes a few times throughout the night, but the delightful memories were worth reliving. Such as the time I jumped into Doctor Commons' arms when I was seven because James Harrington, a big-headed bully from The Manor who only enjoyed finding ways to torture me, was after me again. Doctor Commons was watering his flowers, and I came barreling down towards him as fast as I could like my butt was on fire and leapt into his unexpecting arms which were still able to catch me at the expense of his watering can spilling. Then James, with a big smile that had no front teeth, ran right into Doctor Commons, not being able to stop. I still can see the look on his face as Doctor Commons sat him down in his office and ranted on about proper behavior, after attending to a bruise on James' elbow of course. That was Doctor Commons, protective and headstrong, but caring.

Walking downstairs, I go inside what used to be his bedroom to find some new clothing to wear. My tunic smells pungent, like I took several baths in my own sweat. Finding a shirt and a pair of trousers King Oscar gave him a year ago when they were first introduced, I put them on. The pant legs are a few inches too long so that I'm stepping on them with the soles of my feet, and the shirt looks like I threw a sack on, but despite the fact the outfit is too big for me I make do with it. Finding a pair of shears among an unraveled roll of bandages, I cut off the bottom of portion of my trousers so that I stop stepping on them. Walking barefoot most of the time, I would get quite annoyed always tripping over myself.

Looking for food, I only get greeted by rats as big as cats and roaches that huddle together over every food source. All I find is a bottle of mead. Even that has much to be desired, smelling like a rotten apple tree. It goes down my throat like a moldy stew. Beggars can't be choosers, I suppose.

"To the farms! We are under attack!" cries a soldier outside.

The rattling of an army carriage flies by the door. Running outside, I gaze down the street. The carriage is already skidding around the street corner into city-square. Bolting after it, I stop. Soldiers, hundreds of them, are running hastily outside the city. Following their direction, I weave in and out of the smaller back roads that eventually lead to the North Gate. Sneaking outside by blending with the crowd, I hide behind a bush far enough away from the North Gate that no one will see me, but I can see perfectly fine.

Rebels, too many to count, flood into the farm area from the woods in the far distance. From where I am at, they look like an army of ants with swords, spears, and bows. War cries echo all around like they are everywhere. The guards posted outside the wall stand no chance against the army of rebels. Explosions tear through the farm land. Waving torches around like flags, the rebels set the fields ablaze. Farmers flee from their houses and their families scatter looking like insects fleeing from crows. Mad crows with weapons. They swarm them, swooping down upon the fleeing insects and snatching them up. Blood pours out onto the farm road. Shrill cries pierce the sky. Both royal men and peasants cry together suffering as one. They're safe ground has become a war zone.

From the North Gate comes five wagons full of soldiers. They jump off as soon as they can with weapons drawn. Charging the rebels, the soldiers run in formation. The army of blood hungry crows cross paths with the weasels. Slashing and clawing, they bite and eat each other, using their weapons at hand like teeth and talons. Frantically flying around, the rebels have no formation. They are a wild ball of energy just like the wild fire around them while the soldiers fall into formation protecting the remaining survivors and the North Gate. Raging, the fire expands consuming the small huts along the field edges. Large clouds of smoke cover the landscape. Hectic, the rebels dart around slaying anyone who interferes with them. Some of them wear makeshift armor from iron or leather, but there are plenty of them that wear nothing besides loin cloths, looking like wild savages. The rebels push the soldiers backwards, forcing their line to falter. Taking advantage of the situation, the rebels directly attack the weakest formation, breaking it apart and exposing an open hole in their line. Hollering, a nearby general sends a small group of soldiers away from the North Gate and into battle against the winning rebels. Reinforcements quickly return to the North Gate from inside the city.

Those who use to live inside The Manor probably regret kicking the townspeople to the side. Drinking, dancing, late night parties all had their course, but were the few short years of luxury worth it? Were they worth the miles of blood spilt across the city? No. I'm certain the wealthy, who are now poor, wish they could go back and change their fates. It's too late, though. The few farmers and refugees who survive rush inside the city being escorted by soldiers. Those who don't are brutally beaten to death, beheaded, or to a certain extent raped. Blood fills the beaten farm road. Every divot is now a crimson puddle.

Regaining control, the soldiers push the rebels back. The soldiers strengthen their line and have saved who they could. All they have left to do is protect their city. Sweating, I can feel the heat of the fire. It scorches the battlefield. Noticing how intense the heat has gotten, the rebels come together and flee back into the woods before it is too late. Their bloody attack is through.

Gathering together, the soldiers, with shoulders hunched over and blood stains on their armor, count off. Looking out over the burning fields, I see thousands of bodies and know they will not count off very many. The place looks like a bloody purgatory made by the Devil himself. I can still hear the shrill cries of death in my ears. Weeping, undoubtedly, those who survived will be left crying many nights ahead, just as I will have dreams of this moment. This scarring moment. Blood fills the farm road, but tears flood the city. Marching inside, the soldiers prepare to close the gates. There is nothing out here to save. Running, I quickly get inside before the gate closes. No one notices me. Not a word is expressed and not a soldier makes a sound. There is silence besides the rhythmic marching of the soldiers' feet as they create their wall again between the east and west side. I run back to Doctor Commons' place because certainly The Manor is where all the survivors will stay, and I would rather not listen to hundreds of people weeping at once, crying out for their lost children, parents, husbands, and wives. I'd much rather avoid all that and sleep at Doctor Commons' place. At least then I can hear my own thoughts. Do I really want to hear those? We are all suffering now, and soon we are all going to be starving as well. The clock strikes twelve.

Chapter 35

A thick black cloud, a dark ominous mist, rises over the city. It spreads across the sky cloaking the charred farm land. It towers above everything, rising to the heavens above. Swallowing everything in darkness, it reaches down towards city-square wrapping its fingers around the gallows. Then like a fog, it extends from the gallows consuming every street. Each and every person caught on the streets grow feathers and in a flurry of wings scatter about as crows. Taking part in cannibalism, they tear each other apart, spilling blood across the black streets. Crimson blood mingles with the thick mist.

It becomes so dark, I cannot see a thing. Wading through void, I smell nothing but pungent death. My nostrils curl and my skin burns. Passing through hell itself, I fall deeper into the darkness. Deeper and deeper I fall. Silent. I don't raise a voice. Eerie silence. Feathers brush by my face. They are stiff, flightless, and smell rotten. Deeper I fall. Deeper.

"Thomas!" an echo resounds throughout the dark mist. Spinning around, I feel weightless, but I see nobody. It is far too dark. "Thomas!" I see nobody, but I feel like I am rising out of the mist. Rising out of the darkness. I am no longer sinking. "Thomas!" My eyes blink and flutter open. They must have been closed.

"Thomas!" my father cries, shaking me awake. Rubbing my eyes, I open them to see him standing over me with a firm grip on my head and shoulder. Teeth bared, he has sweat pouring down his flushed face.

"Hello," I mumble.

"Get your sorry hide up to The Manor," he says, throwing me out of bed. Landing on the hard floor with a thud, I moan. My back cracks and my elbows feel tender.

"Why?"

"The city is no longer safe, and they could use your help up there anyway."

Rubbing my arms, I get up. The scars on my back make it impossible to stand straight. Instead, I hunch over. "What is going on?" I ask in between a yawn.

"A battle has been arranged and there is no telling when it may end or how things are going to go. Stay in The Manor."

"Who—"

"Do as you're told!" he bellows, grabbing me by my neck and throwing me up against the wall.

Falling to my knees, I feel light headed. Everything around me sounds distant. My back feels wet. I think my scabs tore open.

"Get up," he says, raising me to my feet roughly.

Stumbling, I head toward the door with terrible pain shooting through my back like it got trampled over by a spooked horse. A carriage awaits outside. The carriage driver throws me into it without a greeting and hurries off. In a blur I am thrown into a crowd of depressed people. Those who lost any will to live. Riding off, the carriage driver leaves behind hundreds of people who cry out to him to take them somewhere. Some cry out for Liberty and others try to run in front of the carriage hoping to be run over. None prevail.

"We'll be safer there they said," says a wiry voice like it is on the edge of a cliff looking down, "We'll be safer there for sure."

Turning around, I see a woman with a rat nest on her head and no clothing on besides what was burned in the fire. Her face is bruised, and her hands are swollen so much so that they look like round tomatoes.

She laughs, saying, "Then in flames falls my child." She looks up at me and smiles saying, "He could have been like you. A fine young man. Could have grown to see the world. He could have before that fire killed him, but do not fear for we are safer there they said." She laughs, biting her nails. Blood leaks from her fingers. Biting on her fingers, she chews on her own flesh. She has no nails to chew.

"I want Mama," cries a little girl down the path I stand on. She sits on a boulder, weeping into her dress. She must be a child of royalty because her dress is made of fine purple silk. Clutched in her fist is a clump of hair. Blond hair unlike hers which is brown. Walking up to her, I notice how puffy her eyes are. They're like bags of pink water. She rubs her face in her dress, pulling it up to her cheeks with the hair in hand.

"Where is your mom?" I ask. I fear she died, but maybe the little girl is just lost.

Staring at me with big, watery eyes, she raises the fist of hair to my face.

"I tried, mister. I tried to pull her back, but that man in his undergarments took her, mister. You know where he is? Can he please give Mama back? Please. After he's done with her inside the farmhouse," she weeps bitterly. Sobbing into her fine purple dress stained with mud and torn at the seams, her face turns bright red.

Dabbing my eye, I sniffle a little, replying, "Do you have other family members around here?"

Grabbing my wrist, she shakes her head vigorously, "No! I only had Mama!"

Clearing my throat, I pull back, walking away.

I can't do this, I think to myself. *I can't handle this.*

Everyone except for a few crazy people seems to huddle together in groups. They mourn together like they are at funerals. Sometimes they scream obscenities for the sake of letting out anger. Others curse the rebels and pray to God that He sends down hell fire upon them like

211

Sodom and Gomorrah, but most of the time they just stand together silently, crying to themselves.

I stand as far as I can from everyone. Hiding behind a boulder, I crouch near the ground, resting my back against it. My head hurts and my muscles ache. I cannot deal with people right now. Especially suicidal people. Then again, how am I much better?

Closing my eyes, I let my body relax.

I can feel the sun on my legs as a shadow protects my face. Feeling drowsy, I slowly sink into sleep. I'm on the verge of passing into a realm absent from time, but before I do, I hear a faint voice in my ear.

"Mister," says the gentle voice. Looking over my shoulder, I see the same little girl in her purple dress.

"Yes," I reply.

"May I sit with you?" she asks, playing with the bottom of her dress between her fidgety fingers. Her pretty eyes that are larger than the stars in the sky investigate mine with hope. Her dusty cheeks with water lines running through them cast a melancholy but beautiful look over her visage.

I nod, saying with a faint smile, "Yes."

Smiling, she huddles close to my side, nuzzling her way under my arm. She must be only seven or eight. Pulling my arm around her, she grabs it gently with her cold fingers which still hold onto that same blond clump of hair. Resting her head against my chest, she sighs with contentment.

Looking at the corner of the wall before us, she whispers, "I miss Mama."

I nod, "I know."

"She's not coming back. Is she?" she asks in the saddest voice, but one with a trace of hope that even though she knows the answer, she wishes that I will say yes.

"No, I'm afraid not," I say.

"That's what I thought." Pulling herself closer to me, she closes her eyes.

212

"Mister."

"Yes."

"Do you have a mama?"

I shake my head, "No, I do not."

Looking up at me with her big brown eyes, she asks, "What happened?"

Clearing my throat, I hold back a tear fighting its way to the corner of my eye. Clearing my throat, I croak, "She died giving birth to me."

"Oh. So, you never met her?"

"No."

"I never met my dad," she says, looking back at the corner of the wall.

"Why's that?" I ask.

"I was a baby when he left. My mom remarried, but her new husband died due to a fever when I was just two."

"Oh," I say.

Sniffling, she wipes her tears with my shirt that I stole from Doctor Commons' closet.

"I miss Mama," she cries, burrowing her face deeper into my shirt.

Hugging her, I brush her dirty hair with my fingers, whispering softly in her ear to calm her. I feel as though it is not my position to do so as I too am suffering. After her spell of tears, she falls asleep in my arm with her head against my chest. I can still feel her tears on my shirt, but I don't mind. I hold her tighter to make sure she's warm and doesn't get cold. Her and I both relate. We both lost parents, and because of that I feel a strange, older brother attachment to her, like for now I should keep her safe. As she sleeps soundly in my arm, I whisper to her, "Don't worry this will all soon be over."

Or so I hope, I think to myself.

Chapter 36

It's early in the morning. Many are sleeping. All those who used to be in royalty made sure they laid claim upon the nice beds inside the little homes. All the plebeians had to fend for themselves finding random spots of grass or marble paths to rest on. I made sure I got my spot in the corner again. Lying in my arm, sleeping, is the little girl with the purple dress whose name I learned to be Faith. Yesterday, she followed me wherever I went as I acted as her older brother making sure she ate, didn't talk to weird strangers, or in some cases warded off men with unhealthy intentions. The more I defended, her the more she clung to me. Even before we went to sleep, she told me I am her new favorite person, which is rather endearing.

Now I lie awake. Gazing at the brilliant stars, I wonder if it is possible to live on a star. Many astrologists have their theories about stars. Some think they are other worlds, some gods, and others simply bright lights just like our sun. Whatever the case may be, I believe there's someone out there. I believe there's another world. I have no proof of course, but this world would seem quite ugly if it was the only one that existed. Living on a dying earth in a dying kingdom seems quite useless; I'd say even a waste of time. I was told, mostly by my father, our kingdom will last forever because there is none like it. I never believed him, but I suppose I thought it wouldn't end like this. Maybe it still won't, but by looking around there isn't much hope.

A shooting star streaks across the night sky. I breathe a silent wish that things will return to how they used to be. Another figure soars overhead. It is darker and much slower and oddly shaped I scrunch my eyes. It is too dark to get a good look at it. Losing velocity, whatever it is it's gets bigger. Sitting up, I wake Faith.

"What?" she mumbles. It comes crashing down landing with a thud on top of my father's house. Another one comes flying over. The catapults! Scrambling to my feet, I start screaming.

"Get up! Get up!" I cry, cupping my hands around my mouth to amplify my voice. Sleeping, many lie on the streets somehow unaware of the two boulders that already struck the earth. Shaking, the ground rocks me back and forth. Behind me another boulder lands on the marble path, shattering it. Waking up, the crazy woman right beside the fallen boulder examines it with a bewildered look.

"What the hell!" she exclaims.

Another boulder comes flying over.

"Watch out!" I scream, but she doesn't even budge.

Crushing her, the boulder sticks into the patch of ground she lied on.

"Thomas!" Faith cries.

"Over here!" I shout back.

Running over to me, she jumps into my arms, sobbing.

"Don't leave me," she cries.

Patting her head, I look around like I can see spirits; people are only slowly getting up.

"Get up!" I scream, running around to each person I find. Most don't seem to understand what's going on.

I hear a cry of anguish from across The Manor. Awaking, more people start to stand up like they are waking from nightmares.

"What's going on?" asks a boy probably only a few years younger than me. I can hardly make out his face, but he is shaking horribly like a flimsy twig. He knocks his knees together like cymbals and looks at me for an explanation. An explanation he knows is not good.

"We are under attack. Get out of here," I say, hoping to come across courageous, but the shakiness in my voice is impossible to mask.

Without another word, he runs like the world depends on it. Some more follow him, only in small packs. There are still a couple here and there who must be heavy sleepers because they still lie on the ground. I spot one on her back, refusing to flee. Her hands are across her breasts and her legs are sprawled out. With her eyes closed, she ignores all the noises around her.

"Get out of here," I tell her. I'm probably red in the face from screaming and carrying Faith around who still wipes her large tears in my shoulder.

"Just let me die," she replies without opening an eye.

"What?"

"All my children were slaughtered, and my husband was burned. Just let me die," she says with a solemn voice.

"For yourself then," I plead.

"They were all I got. Go! Save yourself."

Biting my lip, I set Faith down. Bending over, I try to slide my hands under the woman's back. Considering I am as weak as a lame mule, I probably won't succeed at lifting her, but I try anyhow. Clawing my face, she hisses at me and squirms back onto the ground.

"Let me be," she says, slithering farther away from me. I can hear people dying behind me and can only imagine she will be next.

Faith tugs at my shirt, whimpering.

"I want out of here," she says, reaching her arms out for me like a drowning person.

Picking her back up, I look around. Both exits, the carriage one and the regular ivory one, are now crowded with people well aware of the danger as more boulders crash into The Manor. One lands in the center of the

217

crowd at the ivory gate, knocking several people over like saplings and squashing others like bugs. Bloody screams and wails hammer my ears giving me a headache. Many women fall to their knees over whomever got struck by the boulder. Some parents and other spouses. Only a few men do the same. Many of the men grab their remaining family members and keep pushing forward. They look like lions trying to get through an anthill.

"I know a better way out," I say. Running with Faith in hand, I open a door that leads to the marble hallway circling The Manor. I guess living in The Manor as a kid payed off. Coming to a window I know well because of its distinct red hue, I slam my elbow against it. Shattering, glass slivers dig into my arm. I groan trying to ignore the pain. Being ever so careful, I help Faith outside, dropping her onto the ground where the least amount of glass is. Then squirming out the window, I feel glass shards cut my stomach and tear my clothes. Blood soaks my elbow and bleeds through my shirt. I fall onto the crunchy ground made up of glass. Picking Faith up, who is on the verge of tears, I run.

Beating against my chest, my heart tries to keep up with my feet. I sweat terribly. I don't know where I am running or where it is safe. Shouts echo in the distance. Sounds of bloody war. I can hear horses with bits in mouths exerting all they got against the enemy only to be the first to perish. So, I stay near the wall, as far as I can be from city-square. Faith, sobbing, tears at my bloody shirt with her fingernails. She muffles her wails with my shoulder as I lose stamina.

I must rest, I think to myself.

Collapsing, I drop Faith so that she rolls away from me. Her crying has softened. It is more of a whimper now. Crawling over to me, she observes the state I am in. Blood is everywhere, bruises mask my face, and my clothes are torn to ribbons from glass, nails, and whatever else tore at me. Maybe a branch and maybe a sword. Panting, I hear my own breathing. It is raspy and dry. It sounds awful, like I am dying. My head beats with my heart, but it is a painful beating like someone is knocking the inside of my head with a club. Going numb, my legs twitch along with my fingers and toes. Doctor Commons, if still alive, would certainly have me lie down on his patients' bed and give me medicine; however, Austin, the Devil himself if I may say so, killed him over power lust.

"Curses," I mumble under my breath.

"Thomas, are you OK?" Faith asks, sniffling.

"Yes, I just need to rest," I reply weakly.

Crawling to the side where my arms are, she wiggles her way underneath them. It is warm outside, luckily, but that does not make one feel much better lying helpless out in the middle of nowhere.

Where are we? I ask myself in my head.

Glancing around, all I see is stony dirt and a few bottles. There is a pale hand sticking out of the ground at my feet. Next to it is a small mountain of bodies. We are at The Pit. I hold back my tears. I want to cry because I heard a voice in my head. I swear I did. I swear I heard a voice in my head tell me this is where everyone will be buried, including me. I cry till I fall asleep.

Chapter 37

I had a dream. I can't remember what exactly, but I did. Something with riding on a wagon. Something of that sorts. Waking, I still feel weak. Soaked in blood, my clothes stick to my body. Pangs of pain reside in my gut. My back kills. My body just aches all around, but I can move. Moving my arms, I wrap them tighter around Faith, but I feel nothing. Opening my eyes even more, I look at my arms. There is nobody. She must have gotten up, but that isn't like her to go somewhere without me. Granted I only knew her for a day or two, but we became like brother and sister so quickly. Lowering my arms, I don't feel stony dirt as I expected; I feel cobblestone. Sitting up, I groan. Looking around, I see others lying around me on makeshift mattresses made from hay and rope. Scratching my arm, I feel itchy all over now with hay sticking out of my mop of hair.

Everyone else around me smells of sweat and blood. Some are strong men, men obviously made for war, and others are just plain women. They all are sleeping, however. Around us is a tent made of cotton canvas. Getting up, I walk out the entrance where it parts like a tear in a page of a book. It is located at the very end of the tent. Walking outside, I find myself on the main road leading to city-square which is only a few steps away. Heavily guarded, even more men form a wall in front of the east side. However, I also see that the rebels have formed their own wall as well. They do not look as professional, but they look deadly, nonetheless.

In the center are two people meeting together. The one is a rebel and another a general, and by the look of his build and stance the general is my father. They exchange looks. I can only see Austin's which chills my bones while also boiling my blood. Filled with both rage and fear, I want to claw his eyes out and yet run away from him as far as I can. An odd sensation.

"General Damon," Austin says loudly. He speaks this way so his men may hear him.

"Austin," my father says just as loud.

"Surprised you know my name."

"I know the names of all my enemies."

"Glad I made the list, tyrant."

Shifting his weight onto one leg, my father brings his hands together, cracking his neck; this is something I only see him do when he really must keep a professional posture even though he does not want to. Centering his weight again, he replies, "As of now, you are the list."

"That is quite surprising. I thought an ugly bastard like you would have more enemies. Like Liberty for instance. Aren't they on their way?"

"We have them under control."

"Oh, really? Tis quite strange considering I got word you lost your last three battles."

"Those words are mistaken."

"Maybe, but it does not change who you are."

Stepping closer, my father straightens his back to prove his dominance being a few inches taller than Austin.

"Is that so? And who am I? Certainly not a superstitious plebian who worships crows and takes advantage of young daggle-tails. Those not yet of age."

Laughing to himself, Austin throws back his head like it is not connected to the rest of his body. Sort of like a puppet. Then he snaps forward with a jolt and ceases his laughter, "You have no understanding. The Beast will devour you."

"Certainly hope not considering I am looking at him."

"Me? You must be mad. A loony. I am the future of this city."

"You are its demise."

"*You* are its demise. I am its savior."

"You abhorrent jackass!" my father bellows, shaking now. I see his hand twitching above the hilt of his sword. Noticing this, Austin laughs.

"Touchy, are we? Look, if you are truly a general, prove it."

"A battle."

"Where?"

"Right here."

"When?"

"Starting tomorrow."

"Morning?"

"Mornings and evenings. The afternoons are far too hot."

"So, giving us both a respite."

"Precisely."

"Agreed." Shaking on it, they both walk back to their men.

With a great scowl across his face, my father shoves his men out his way and walks up the main road. Walking so he can think.

"Thomas!" Faith exclaims, throwing her arms around my waist. I wince, but I try to cover it with a smile. With a frown she apologizes, "Sorry."

"It is all right," I say, hugging her back.

"I was looking for you in my tent on the other side of the street. Then I saw you."

"Glad you are safe."

Looking over at all the soldiers, her face creases.

"What is happening?"

Frowning, I reply, "War, Faith. War."

"People are going to die like my mom?"

Nodding silently, I think of that day. The fields consumed in flames as those crows and weasels fought each other. As they scraped at each other accomplishing nothing except more death. More peril. More heartbreak. Leaving a girl like Faith motherless.

"I'm scared," Faith whimpers.

"So am I," I say.

So am I.

Chapter 38

The sun awoke this morning to witness bloodshed. What has the sun seen in this land he didn't approve of? How often does he wake and cry over the hopeless? How often does he serve as an audience member to a show of destruction?

An audience, I suppose that's what we are. Austin and Damon both have those not participating in the battle, which are mostly women and children, sit in rows across the main road. Of course, the rebels sit on the west side of the city as I and the others sit on the east side. This morning guards file us out of our tents and sit us down. Of course, as fate would have it, I get a front row seat right next to Faith. That is exactly what a little girl should witness — more death. Certainly, a brilliant idea to give her a clear view of the spectacle. Holding my hand, she trembles. She knows what is about to happen. This is not a normal battle. This is a battle of small proportions. Lines of soldiers surround us meant to protect us from attacks. Archers stand on top of buildings and will only fire if the civilians are under siege. City-square, where the battle is meant to be fought, will be a sea of death. Marching in front of his men, my father numbers off about fifty men. As they are called, they step out from the line of well-equipped soldiers. Austin does the same. He has managed to find a way to receive a small contribution of armor to make the battle fairer. Since the battle is mostly under my father's terms, he lent Austin armor. That was my father's decision. King Oscar is just one of us now. He was dethroned a couple days ago. However, if this battle fairs well for my father, King Oscar will get his throne back. I'm sure of it. He always had his way with words. Flattery mostly.

Marching in line, the selected soldiers face the rebels' disjointed line like a man with leprosy. General Damon stands behind his men, far enough to not be included, but close enough to be heard.

"Ready yourselves!" he orders.

Instantly, the fifty men all have their swords drawn and shields ready. They are quite amazing to watch in how perfect they are at performing their job, which some would consider an art. The art of warfare. A bloody art with its only beauty hidden in the soldiers themselves in how they fight and move. Sort of like acrobatics, but their intent is not to entertain.

"Slaughter them!" Austin growls. Pulling out spears, swords, and even a couple battle axes, the rebels are not nearly as organized. Some people are much slower than others at drawing their weapons, and one even fights with his sheath as he tries to draw his sword. It is a show. I nearly laugh, but the intensity in the air keeps my mouth shut. The air is too thick to breathe.

Sliding closer to me, Faith whispers, "Now I'm really scared."

I nod, "I know. I know."

A horn resounds from one of the roofs on the east side. Charging forward, the soldiers holler as one unit, creating a sound like thunder. It is powerful. Screaming in spurts, the rebels have no unity. They are fighting for themselves; they are simply crows flying around for their own gain. Yet I can't say the soldiers have the moral high ground; they are called weasels for a reason.

Two seconds. Two seconds of peace. Loud peace, but peace until the first clash of the blade. A clash which sliced through the air itself cutting everybody, even those watching. At the end of this war there will be a winner and a loser. How many will be left is hard to say. Faith tightens her grip on my hand.

Slashing, the rebels are very unorthodox. They obviously have been training, but not trained to play by the rules; they are trained to break them. Taking advantage of the soldiers' rigid ways, the rebels catch the soldiers off guard. Ramming their sides into the soldiers, the rebels lunge forward, swinging for heads. Only two soldiers succumb to this surprising tactic; most bounce back into action, remembering their training. A rebel with an iron spear pierces the throat of a soldier, but the rebel's failure to watch his sides led to a sword beneath his arm and across his thigh. Burrowing her face into my shoulder, Faith whimpers. She is trying to muffle her cries.

Grunting, a large man with a gut belonging to an elephant swings a battle axe around keeping many at bay, but his lack of agility leads to his death as a soldier runs behind him, catches his lower leg with his sword, then pounces upon the back of his neck. The soldiers are winning. Twenty-four soldiers and fourteen rebels remain. It is practically two against one. Grouping together, the rebels create a moon formation, their first real strategy. Those with shields hold them out in front of them and those without just hold out their weapons. Accustomed to such formations, the soldiers get into a line holding out their shields that protect their entire midsections and torsos. Closing in, they keep their swords drawn, wrapping around the rebels.

Lunging forward, the rebels dive at the legs of the soldiers. Some rebels succeed at knocking some soldiers over, but most fail miserably. Screams and blood fill city-square, and a pile of bloody rebels are left behind. Tight against me, like she is nailed into my side, Faith presses her face into my shoulder, refusing to watch. Her blindness does not protect her ears which can hear every moan and cry for help. She trembles whenever such cries are let out, and she squeezes my hand tighter. So tight sometimes I'm afraid I'll lose my fingers. Yet I can't blame her. War is no game, and death brings no joy.

Cursing, Austin rips out patches of his long, shaggy hair. He has not trimmed for a long time. Sitting on a chair wearing chains around her wrists and ankles with gray and black hair hanging down the side of her face is who I can only guess was the woman with beautiful black hair. Now she is far from beautiful. Sitting next to Austin, who paces back and forth haughtily, she doesn't move. Doesn't speak. She is motionless with black feathers wrapped around her head like a halo. A halo made for one of Satan's angels. Seemingly possessed, she spews over with an aura of evil despite the fact she doesn't move an inch. Yet something tells me if I turned my back on her, she would have my throat in a second. From what I can see, bruises blacken her face even more than the makeup she wears above her eyes. She has been transformed from a beauty to a horrible beast. Chained to Austin forever.

"Do you want to continue this battle? I have many more soldiers to kill your puny men," taunts my father.

"No, we will fight again. Get your half-witted asses to clean this disgrace before we continue," he replies, pointing at the dead bodies, or those nearly dead. The two drunks quickly but unsteadily use horses to pull a large wagon through the North Gate to throw the bodies in until they are ready to be buried, which may be a while. Considering how well the drunks work, it may never happen. The drunks already have their jugs on the wagon just in case they get thirsty.

After all the bodies are clumsily thrown into the wagon, the drunks ride outside the city walls to park the wagon until after the next battle and the next and the next. Until afternoon time. In each battle, the soldiers have the upper hand. They only lose one out of the four battles. Austin, understandably, is enraged from watching his men die. Not because he cares about them necessarily, but because that means he is losing to Damon, his greatest enemy.

For the afternoon, the people are forced back into the two tents they came from. Faith follows me, of course, like a scared puppy follows its master in a crowd. Holding onto the back of my torn shirt, she trails me closely. All afternoon we have to stay in the tents for our own security, which means a lot of naps for me and Faith because we both refuse to interact with others. For hours we stay together napping and talking until evening comes. Then in orderly fashion, we all sit where we were in the morning to watch the evening fights.

Great, more death, I think to myself.

Nothing has changed besides my father's pride, which swells every battle. The evening is a repeat of the morning, leading to an onslaught of brutal remarks from my father's lips intended for Austin who is steaming. Face red and knuckles white, he curses back without restraint.

"You should surrender before your army becomes a graveyard," my father scoffs from where he sits. He orders someone to bring him a wooden stool which he gloats in after every victory. Using it almost as a thrown, he even sips on a glass of wine. He reminds me of Troy. Troy is seated beside the woman who use to have beautiful black hair; his cold, beady black eyes throw daggers at Damon. Falling quickly, the sun is fading away and the night grows in strength.

"We continue tomorrow," Austin says before ripping through his audience back to wherever he stays. Damon snorts, marching through his own audience. These two great forces will not give up until one of them dies. Pride is their downfall.

Chapter 39

Like a pack of wolves, the rebels snarl and bark as they tear apart the fallen soldiers. Digging their teeth into the soldiers' arms, necks, and even their legs. The rebels use the arms from corpses like clubs and hack off the soldiers' limbs. Dwindling quickly like the last drops of water in a glass, the soldiers fall back, completely unprepared for such a rabid pack of men. All night I could hear men and women chanting. Crows were cackling and children were laughing maniacally, and to no one's surprise Crow Mother was among the rebels' audience today. She is exactly in the middle of the crowd watching with a crooked grin.

It is five to forty. A complete massacre. Never has such uncontrollable rage been witnessed. The rebels' fighting style is animalistic. In their hair are feathers like headdresses made for Egyptian kings, and war paint like blood coats their arms and legs. They howl and growl all at the same time, curdling my blood. My stomach is sick. Today, Faith must sit in my lap smothering her face into my chest. Her back faces the battle. I want to do the same, but I would never get away with it. Watching with utter terror, I remember meeting Crow Mother. I remember her claws digging into Doctor Commons. She moved and flew about just like a hellion. That is exactly how the rebels are fighting, and my father has never looked more horrified. Today he is not gloating. Standing, he watches with wide eyes. I should have warned him that their black magic is no joke.

Without restraint, the forty rebels surround the soldiers and beat them. Taking away the soldiers' weapons, the rebels pile on top of them like vultures and tear them apart without using weapons. Screaming out of terror, the five soldiers can be heard begging for mercy, which is unheard of for soldiers. They are taught to be brutally strong, but they snapped. Gasping, the audience behind me can be heard whispering and children crying. A cloud of horror has dissipated across us all. The sun can't even watch! It has covered its face with a dark cloud.

"That is enough, you *monsters*!" my father bellows, grabbing the stool he got yesterday and splintering it against the ground.

Laughing hysterically, Austin grabs his sides.

"Prepare for more like that," he hoots.

Getting up with fresh blood running down their faces, necks, and arms, the forty remaining rebels gather together in a circle and howl. They all have painted eyes on their foreheads and claw marks across their cheeks, just like Doctor Commons. I shudder.

"I refuse to watch such disgusting foul play," my father says, stepping out to city-square. "This is a battle, not a place for caged animals."

Still laughing, Austin replies, "So do you surrender? If so, you have less back bone than I thought."

"Of course not. I demand more chivalry."

"Chivalry is a word used by cowards. If you refuse to fight on, you accept defeat, which under the terms of our agreement means *I* take power."

"Dammit! We fight on," my father says, stomping back to his men. "The next fifty get out there, and forget the code of war. Murder those ugly bastards."

Silence falls upon the crowd; this will no longer be a battle, but a blood bath. It will be a fight between animals finding any way possible to kill each other. The rules of survival. Weasels versus crows.

Getting into formation after the dead bodies are cleaned up, the next fifty face each other. At the first command, the soldiers run forward with no code of chivalry holding them back. Lunging into each other, both sides are doing anything possible to get an advantage. Flapping about wildly, the rebels use diversions as a large part of their strategy. They run around and flap their arms, then when the soldiers don't know what to do, that's when the rebels fly forward with deadly blows and jabs. Using much more of their strength, the soldiers now use less swordsmanship as in classical wars and use more of their body. Elbowing, punching, and slamming their shields into the enemy, they push their weight forward to keep the rebels from creating diversions. Growling, barking, howling, and whooping can be heard all across the city. Sobbing, Faith pulls so hard at my shirt she puts more tears into it. Yet I hardly notice because all my attention is on the battle. The battle of beasts. Ripping and beating each other, they look like demons. It is almost like hell decided to open its gates and let its inhabitants duke it out right in the middle of our city, if it can even be called a city anymore considering nearly half our population died due to this war. Maybe even more considering Liberty is still at war with us. Within a day or two, we will certainly be nothing but a pile of ash. We will no doubt go down in history as the city of death. Our own people kill each other.

Becoming a lake of blood, city-square no longer is a bland gray, but a deep crimson. With each step the soldiers or rebels take, they splash around in puddles of blood, spraying their legs with the nasty fluid. Wearing nothing on their feet, the rebels' feet are soaked in blood which must seep into their heads because that's all they seem to desire anymore. Their eyes are filled with hate. Burning hatred. Maybe they are from hell. Yet at this point the soldiers look no better as they growl like dogs.

Picking up an arm, a rebel beats the final remaining soldier who is on his knees. He strikes him again and again until finally the soldier's body falls prostrate. The rebels win again with nine remaining. Silence. Silence falls upon both sides. My father's face has gone pale. Even he, a soldier for most of his life, has never seen such a sight. A sight so brutal and inhuman that not even Austin can laugh. All he can do is grin. Crow Mother is the only one making noise, cackling. Hateful glares are shot her way, but she doesn't care.

"Does Damon want a respite?" Austin asks unable to wipe away his smug grin.

"Yes," my father mutters. Everyone is escorted to the tents.

Evening arrives. Not a soul talked all afternoon, and no one talks now. In my arms is Faith, weeping. Austin and Damon were speaking with each other all afternoon somewhere. I am unsure of the details, but I'm sure it had to pertain with the spectacle in the morning. If I live to be an old man, I will certainly remember this war more than anything else. I am not sure if I will ever sleep again. Lining up, the soldiers and rebels prepare for another battle. Never have I experienced so much fear and suspense.

"Fight," orders my father, but not loudly. It is a tone of reluctance.

With their headdresses flapping in the evening wind, the rebels soar forward. The air is dense not only because of the battle at hand, but also because of a storm to come. There are towering dark clouds in the distance making everything darker than usual. Maybe the sun has seen enough. A loud clap of thunder shakes the ground as the weasels and crows clash. Standing beside Austin, Crow Mother watches intently. An ominous look rests in her eyes. Even Troy, who I only ever saw sitting before, stands with a large cloak on. One that covers his whole body like a baggy brown sack. Everyone on the rebel side seems more on edge. Even some people in the audience are standing. Maybe they are prepared for rain. I can't imagine this battle will be called off because of rain.

An hour or two goes by with the same types of battles as this morning. Getting bigger, the storm expands like God is about to release his wrath. The night gets darker. Everyone on the west side is standing. It must be at least eight at night. It is so dark I cannot see.

"No more!" my father shouts, "It is far too dark."

Austin was about to send out more men for another battle.

"Far too dark?" Austin asks dumbly.

Damon and Austin approach each other.

"Yes. Tomorrow we continue."

"Why must you continue to push off the inevitable?"

"What do you mean?"

"Obviously, I will win. My men have slaughtered yours all day."

"As mine did yours yesterday."

Squinting, I try to see what their expressions are like, but I can't.

"You have gone weak," retorts Austin.

"No, I have not," my father replies with anger swelling in his voice.

"Surrender already."

"We continue this tomorrow," says my father bluntly.

Bellowing, the clouds thunder.

"I'm afraid not," Austin says.

Tearing off his cloak, Troy is lit like a torch. Dashing forward, he screams loudly. Great confusion falls upon everybody until we all can see the grenades tied around his chest and waist. A thin white garment covers his body; the one on fire. The flame has lit the grenades. Leaping out of my chest, my heart stops.

His sable black eyes are lit with vengeance. Freezing, I watch in horror. Doctor Commons' face flashes through my mind. Troy is a vengeful Doctor Commons. I'm in a fear filled daze until Faith's shrill cries awake me. Scooping her up in my arms, I jump over people trying to get as far away as possible. Screaming, everyone scrambles backwards in a mad rush.

"For The Beast!" I hear Troy cry before a terrible explosion splits my ears.

Chapter 40

Ringing. Terrible ringing rips through my head. I fall over from the explosion, dropping Faith. Cracking, my back feels stiff and my joints feel worn down. A terrible migraine eats away at me. Tugging at my arms, Faith screams in my face. Her pretty, tear-filled brown eyes look into mine. Tears trickle down her eyes and cheeks. Flushed red, she tries desperately to get me up. Crawling, I cough hoarsely. I see feet out of the corner of my eye; they are not running away from city-square, but rather towards it. Looking over my shoulder in pain, I see that the whole city is fighting. Something snapped inside everyone. Everybody looks like an animal. Men, women, and children all scream and fight each other. Swarming each other, both sides claw and scratch using whatever they have in hand.

"Let's get out of here!" I hear Faith cry. My hearing is returning.

Cackling above are crows. Flocks of crows. They remind me of the storm cloud which is getting terribly near us. The crows laugh at our madness.

Crawling, I feel weak. Wobbling, my legs knock together as I stand. Faith continues to try to motivate me to hurry. Arrows fly overhead from the buildings surrounding us. The archers have engaged. Another explosion sounds, sending a dozen people flipping through the air.

"Hurry!" Faith shouts. Her voice is on the verge of breaking like cracked glass.

Stumbling, I get knocked back by someone's shoulder. A bunch of people are still rushing city-square. Then I'm knocked down again. Hitting my back against the cobblestone, everything goes black and white. Color patches spot my vision, but otherwise everyone and everything is either black or white. Faith runs my way, but a pair of legs trip over her, bumping her into the ground. My body aches, my head is throbbing, and my vision has gone bad. It feels like all my insides are about to break out and spill across the street.

Clawing the cobblestone, I force myself up with Faith clinging to me. Gazing at city-square, I watch our city's demise unfold. Austin and Damon both are dueling each other with swords. Neither one is able to defeat the other, but they have both managed to somehow destroy themselves. Can they not see the destruction at hand? Women are being beaten by grown men. A baby wails on the ground only to be trampled over by rebels and soldiers alike. Utter chaos. A storm of its own kind. I am so amazed at how blind everyone is to the madness at hand that I fail to notice Faith's absence. Her firm grip on my shirt has weakened. Befuddled, I look down to see her lying on the street with an arrow lodged in her chest.

"Faith!" I cry, falling to my knees.

Her eyes are already glazed over with blank void. A sinkhole of sorts. One that no one ever returns from. Weeping, I cry out her name, but she doesn't respond. I grab her hand, cupping it. Warmth still radiates from it, but it is fading. Her chest moves slightly and slowly.

"Faith!"

Her mouth moves, but only air leaks from her lips. The only air she has left. Raising her other hand to my face, she rubs my cheek gently mouthing what I can only determine to be a thank you. *A thank you for what? Letting her die!*

"Faith no!" I scream.

Falling, her hand hits the cobblestone with a light thud like the feet of a child walking for the first time. Her chest ceases to move.

"Faith!"

Faith has died. Faith has died on my account! Weeping, my eyes burn with tears. Bitter tears. "No! No! No!"

Punching the street, I feel my hand break, but I don't care. I could die right now and I wouldn't care. Scooping Faith into my arms, I cradle her limp body. With tears in my eyes, I journey towards The Pit. *I refuse to leave her on the street*, I think to myself. The Pit is no place to bury such a child, but it is the only place available. It is better than being torn apart by monsters. In between tears, I dig through the stony soil with my hands. I dig until I make enough room to bury Faith. Covering her body, I stare at her face with tears dripping from my cheeks. I look at her knowing oh so well she will never return. I lost Doctor Commons and now her. Although I only knew her a short while, she was the only other person besides Dr. Commons that I can say I loved. And now here she is. Closing my eyes, I cover her face with dirt. Standing, I look down at city-square. Through the dark and with my bad vision, I cannot see much, but I can hear the screams and can only imagine the bloodshed. Wiping my eyes, I march. I march forward knowing oh so well it is to my death I march.

I have nothing left, I think to myself.

City-square gets nearer. Many have already died. The storm has gotten closer. It is thundering loudly. I don't know how much time passed, but by how dark it, is much more time must have passed then I have realized. Yet everything seems irrelevant. I march. Marching to my death. *I have nothing left.*

City-square is only a few paces away. Soon I am swept into the tide of angry men. Swept into the tide of angry women. Swept into the tide of angry children. Swept into the tide of death. Being tossed around, to and fro, I feel nothing at all. I feel no fear, no anger, no sorrow. I feel nothing. Flailing to the ground next to the North Gate, I notice for the first time a sword has been driven into my side. Stuck there.

Midnight strikes. A great flash of lightning burns through the sky, striking outside the gate. Looking over in awe, I see Jonah standing at the gate with his head low. He is leaving.

"Jonah!" I shout. My voice is ragged like an old washcloth.

Looking at me, he frowns.

"Yes."

"Where are you going?" I ask. It is so weird that I ask such a simple question when I am dying, yet I do not care.

Walking over to me, he says, "I'm leaving. That is all."

"The Beast. Is he here?"

Jonah nods, "He is here."

I look at city-square and back at him.

"Where?"

"He surrounds us, and he is consuming us."

"I don't understand," I say.

"Death."

"Death?"

"True death, the one that divides people. The one that isolates then destroys. Even those who think they are strong or have favor succumb to it when the opposite has always been true."

"I still don't understand."

Gazing at city-square, Jonah sighs, "Many do not. Many fight and bicker and blame never to realize The Beast is consuming them. That is true death. Not the death we see when one is buried beneath the dirt. No. True death is when our pride consumes us and, when faced with the reality of our depravity, we fall deeper into its clutches. Deeper into the jaws of The Beast."

240

Struggling to stay focused, I can feel my body beginning to go limp. I cannot understand or comprehend what Jonah is trying to say, but I want to. I want to know what he means. I want to know why. I want to know all I can just to know I died for a reason, or at least with a reason.

Looking at me, Jonah dabs at a tear, "I see that your life is also fading. I wish there was more I could do, but I can only do so much." Jonah now cries, "I am only the message bearer. I feel cursed, like God himself has made me weak. I can only see the message he has, but the solution lies in the hands of others, and those others don't always seek to find truth. Those others don't seek to find God and his Son. Those others merely die at each other's hands. They don't fight The Beast, they just fight each other unaware of the Devil inside."

Tears now are crashing down his face, but I don't understand. I don't understand why. Fading away, my vision is going bad. Darkness closes in around my eyes. I feel rain upon my head pouring down. Jonah begins to walk away. He walks out the gate.

I don't understand. I don't understand, I think to myself, feeling the rain pour down upon me. Holding onto my life, I fight the inevitable. Gasping for air, I cling to every breath. My neck falls; it falls towards the gate. I see a horse. A black horse, but then again everything looks black to me. I see an army. An army stumbling upon our dying city. There is someone in front of the army on the black horse. He wears a crown. I cannot see well. My vision is going blank.

Is that Liberty?

My vision is fading. My hearing has dissipated, and all I can sense anymore is the rain falling upon my head. Tears well up in my eyes.

I don't understand.

I fade away. I melt beneath the rain, but I swear I can feel a hand. A warm hand. Something. Some faint hope. A faint impression. Maybe a cross on a crown, but most certainly a hand. A warm hand. Before I feel nothing at all.

L.T. World is a graduate of Eastern Lebanon County (ELCO) High School in Pennsylvania and a current student at Lebanon Valley College (LVC). He began writing in eighth grade when his English teacher encouraged him to pursue a writing career. Dedicating a lot of time to his practice, L.T. began to submit literature pieces to magazines and publishers during his senior year of high school. Prophesy is his first published novel. When he's not writing, L.T. enjoys reading and spending time with friends. He believes, "The imagination is the canvas for an author."